# Baby Momma

# Baby Momma

Ni'Chelle Genovese

*www.urbanbooks.net*

Urban Books, LLC
78 East Industry Court
Deer Park, NY 11729

ISBN 13: 978-1-60162-661-5
ISBN 10: 1-60162-661-4

First Mass Market Paperback Printing February 2013
First Printing February 2012
Printed in the United States of America

10 9 8 7 6 5 4 3 2

*This is a work of fiction. Any references or similarities to
actual events, real people, living or dead, or to real locales
are intended to give the novel a sense of reality. Any simi-
larity in other names, characters, places, and incidents is
entirely coincidental.*

Distributed by Kensington Publishing Corp.
Submit Wholesale Orders to:
Kensington Publishing Corp.
C/O Penguin Group (USA) Inc.
Attention: Order Processing
405 Murray Hill Parkway
East Rutherford, NJ 07073-2316
Phone: 1-800-526-0275
Fax: 1-800-227-9604

# Acknowledgments

Well, where do I start. I guess at the beginning, because without Him nothing is possible and with Him there is nothing that is impossible—I give the greatest thanks to God. My parents, Cheryl and Haywood Boyd, my brother, Haywood Jr., and my sister-in-law, Tami, my foundation, my support, and the only people who have always understood that with me, an idea is just the beginning. To my grandfather, Clarence Harris, who before passing sat me on his front porch in the country when I was fourteen and told me, "Never listen to anyone. No matter what you do or what people tell you, you make sure you be your own star and make your own way in this world." His advice might have made me eccentric as hell, but success is success! Uncle Kyle—I love you too. The only ears I talk off when I'm going through, Marie Harvey and Gwenetta Gillespie. Huge thank yous to my manager First Tonia, Drew Sidora, and Gina Quintero, you all saw in me what so many others couldn't fathom and I am ever so grateful. Justice Williams for the journey that began with a single step. Harold "H" Willams, Moosh Millz, and Cicely RichGirl, it's a wrap! Dana, Brandy, Shatonda, Natasha M. and Rene Bailey, y'all are my newest inspirations! Jovan, Mark, Richard, Drew, Natasha K. Stephon, and Tomika, my "fam" forever. My Schmidgette's Nene a.k.a. Papi and Tiffany Wynn, I love you both more than words can express, there will always be a special place in my heart and life for you guys. Author Kole Black you are the best! Kiki Swinson, the most successful author and humblest soul I've ever met in my life. Mr. Tracy Marrow a.k.a. Ice T and his better half Coco—Thank you all for the gems that helped me along the way!

—**Ayiesha Ni'chelle**

First and foremost thanks to my mother, Yvetta Tonia, and my kids. Jasmine. Montre. Bryce. Asia. Everything I've ever done or tried to do was for a better life for you guys! Daddy loves you. To my second mother "Pea," worlds of I love you. To my homie Governor Washington and Tee, thank you for everything you have ever done for me. Some of my best times were being on the road with you; you're one of the greatest singers in the world. To Drew Sidora, we had our ups and downs together; thank you for bringing me into your life and showing me a new world. It was a pleasure to say I'm Drew Sidora's manager and friend; I love you, sis, and the Jordan family. My FM/ Bloom Family. ThatguyMark. Kassandra Smith aka Lambo. Atiba. Mike Bless. Thelma Guyton. Velly. Let's start a new chapter with this music and our business. To my partner, Kim Lumpkin. Gina Quintero. Mark, I love you guys, and thank you for helping this book make the light of day! To my two advisors, *Essence* bestselling author Kiki Swinson and hit maker Moosh Millz, you both mean the world to me and words can never express how I feel just writing this, but thank you both. And to Tblack and Sherita Worlds we are family love you! Thank you to Tanya Smith and Keke aka Sis and Momma Smith for always calling me son. From the Hawkins to the Riddicks and Tonia, I love my family and friends 1stGen-Publishing.

—**Maurice First Tonia**

# Thug Passion

## 1

I lay back on the fake leather couch, sippin' my Henny and relaxing while I let Honey take care of me. Honey was the finest stripper at the Hot Spot, one of the few remaining strip clubs in East Ocean View. No one had an ass as big and as soft as hers, and on top of that, the bitch was fine. If she wanted to, she could be in any rap nigga's video, no questions asked. She had cinnamon-brown skin that glowed like she was covered in baby oil twenty-fo'-seven, and these titties that just seemed to hypnotize. I had been fuckin' wit' her for a minute. I came to the club and checked her out, even made it rain like a hurricane lettin' loose tens and twenties all over the stage every now and then. In return, I knew that this was my piece of ass until I decided otherwise. Honey climbed on my lap and leaned close to me. She started to whisper into my ear.

"I missed you, Rasheed. You ain't gave me none in a week."

I gave her my famous boyish grin and playfully whispered back, "You know what to do." And so it began. She reached down between her legs and grabbed the belt of my pants. I had been missing that pussy a li'l bit so I decided to help her get to it a li'l faster. I set my glass down, undid my belt, and pulled out what I liked to call every bitch's bad habit. You see, every nigga thinks he got the biggest dick in the world until he stand beside a nigga wit' a bigga one. I ain't confessin' to peekin' at nobody's Johnson, but I could damn sure say I got that crack rock, dope-fiend, call me Jerry Springer 'cause I'ma leave ya ho sprung type dick!

Honey was definitely addicted. First, she massaged it wit' her hand. I didn't know what this broad be doing wit' her hands, but they were soft as hell and always made me shiver a little bit when she stroked me like that.

I was getting excited as I listened to R. Kelly's "Wind for Me" playing in the background. I grabbed the side strap of her thong and untied it. I could feel it fall apart on my lap and I started to palm her ass. Damn, this bitch had a nice ass. I couldn't even get all of it in my hands, but damn if I wasn't trying.

I suddenly had the urge to feel her wet lips. She wasn't experienced at givin' head. From what she told me, she'd just lost her virginity the year before when she was eighteen. I could believe that shit, 'cause a nigga was a breath away from punchin' her in the top of her too damn expensive Remy weave the first time she ever went there with me. I can't stand feelin' teeth, nails, any of that shit grazin' my dick. I made it a point to teach her 'cause a nigga like me need that shit in my life for sho. Good head *and* good pussy from the same bitch is a hot commodity. You can find a million and one chicks who'll give it to you, but only a handful can do that shit like Pinky the Pornstar or Superhead. I like these young chicks 'cause they got more potential and they definitely more willing to learn. Not that I'm that much older than Honey; five years ain' shit in this day and age.

I grabbed her waist and lifted her off my lap.

She looked a little puzzled, like she didn't understand what was going on. "What's wrong, baby? You want me to stop?" she asked.

I loved her voice. It was kinda hoodish and whiny, but still sexy in that young chick kinda way.

"Naw, girl, I just want to watch you suck that shit for me."

"But, baby, what if somebody see me? I could get fired." She really sounded like she was worried about it.

Somebody needed to remind her that I owned the fucking club. We were secluded in the smaller one of three lounge areas. They were primarily for private dances but every now and again someone would rent a section for a bachelor party or whateva. I had already requested this section be reserved and undisturbed, so Honey was worrying for no reason.

Besides, the only person with the audacity to even go against my word in here was my biz partner Derrick, and last time I checked he was busy tryin'a holla at a new bitch who came in yesterday lookin' for work. She looked a li'l old in the face by my standards, but she had an hourglass, wide-body physique that left a nigga speechless! Shit, with the right makeup and lighting we could pull in stupid paper off her shifts for sure.

I smacked Honey on her ass, gave her a little grin, and told her to get to work. She hesitated for a second, then got on her knees and started her practice test. She was getting better. I felt less teeth, and damn, this shit was starting to feel real good. I had to grab her head a couple of times to stop her 'cause I didn't want to bust in her mouth. I wanted to feel that pussy tonight.

"Come here, baby, come fuck daddy real good," I told her and obediently she did.

She straddled my lap and placed me inside her. It felt like a warm cloud had surrounded me. With every movement she made, every up and down stroke, I felt my legs go weak. I didn't know what it was this broad had in there but that shit was like heaven. And she was so willing to do whatever I asked.

I could get that shit anywhere I wanted. Maybe the fact that I was the biggest drug dealer in the city had something to do with it. They can deny 'til they die but every bitch wants a li'l excitement. A li'l rush of adrenaline when you see ya nigga. These bullshit-ass playas talkin' 'bout they runnin' game and doin' shit big. Connect four hustlas, 'cause that's how many times they product gets chopped down before it ever even touches they hands. I'm number fuckin' one. Runnin' this fast-paced, do-or-die shit that a regular nigga or Reggie, as I like to call 'em, too scared to do. Single, married, young, old, it don't matter. Bitches just naturally gravitated to a nigga like me.

I could hear Honey's breath gettin' raspy as our bodies molded together. I loved the way she stared me directly in the eyes while she was gettin' it. That shit was like a silent challenge, sayin' a nigga needed to go deeper or stroke harder. If her eyes closed even for an instant I knew I was hittin' it *extra right*. She grabbed my hand, placed my pointer finger in her mouth, and began to suck it as if it were my dick. Talk about some sexy shit. She must have been watching those porno tapes I left for her the other day. I could tell she studied 'em hard 'cause she was working my ass. I might have to hit this shit again before the night was over with.

Just as I was getting ready to let go, I was distracted by my phone vibratin' in my pants pocket against my ankle. I leaned forward, placed my arm around Honey's waist so she wouldn't fall, and I grabbed my phone. It was Michelle, my baby momma. Leanin' back against the couch, I gave Honey a nod to keep going and answered the phone.

"What's up?"

"Rasheed, where are you? It's almost two-thirty in the morning."

Michelle was pissed. I had told her I'd be home at eleven. She hated it whenever I'd show up later than expected, even after I told her I didn't like bein' asked that type of shit in the first place. Michelle was always clockin' a nigga. If it took fifteen minutes to get home from somewhere and I got there in twenty, she'd be right there at the front door with all sorts of questions and accusations. Actin' like I actually stopped for five minutes to fuck anotha bitch or somethin'.

"I'm handling some very important business right now, an' I'm a li'l busy. I'll be there, damn."

Honey shifted and rode me harder, excitin' me and makin' me address Michelle more aggressively than I meant to.

"Well, your son has a fever, jackass, and he needs to go to the hospital. You need to come on."

It killed me when she tried to tell me what the fuck to do. She knew damn well that I wasn't gonna get there until I was ready. "Well, I guess you need to make a trip to the hospital then. I'll be there." I ended the call before she could respond.

Honey had already cum. I could feel her wetness running down my leg, but being the good girl she was, my baby was going to ride until daddy told her to stop. That's why I liked these young broads. You dick 'em up real good, throw 'em a few dollars, get their hair and nails done, maybe take 'em out to eat, and they happy. Michelle almost fucked up my mood, but all I had to do was look at Honey's pretty face and get a feel of that ass and I was right back where I had been sixty seconds ago.

I forced my hips upward, slammin' into her each time she thrust down. I knew she liked it when I did that, and I could see ecstasy written all over her face. She grabbed my shirt and the more she grabbed the harder I rammed into her. When she couldn't take it anymore, she grabbed the back of my neck and loosened her legs around me. That was my cue to take over. I pulled her closer, focusin' on my breathing so I'd last longer. The scent of musky leather from the overused couch mingled with Honey's signature Juicy Couture sweetness pushin' me closer to the edge. I was startin' to feel like a taut rubber band extended to the max and ready to pop. Instinct took over and I started fuckin' the shit outta her. I was gonna make sure her ass wasn't gettin' back on stage tonight.

When I thought I was about to pass out more from the pleasure than the pain, I let myself give in and I exploded in a heated flood of pleasure and muscle spasms.

"Damn girl, you gonna make me stalk yo' ass if you keep puttin' it down like that."

"Oh really, well wait 'til daddy see what else I learned."

She got up from my lap and bent down over my dick. She placed it in her mouth and licked it clean. Damn, she was surprising the hell out of me tonight. I'd have to find out what she really been up to.

She stood up and gave me a kiss on the cheek. I smacked her on her ass and told her to go get dressed 'cause we were leaving. She ran to the dressing room, no questions asked, and I headed to the car to wait for her.

I had thought about going straight to the hospital to meet Michelle, but I couldn't get rid of Honey tonight. I was too hot and too ready and Michelle had given me too much lip. I didn't even want to touch her ass tonight. She would just have to wait until tomorrow to see me, and that was only if she didn't piss me off again. I cringed as Honey hopped into the passenger side of my all-white Lexus LFA. Three oily smudges skewed my view out the passenger side window from where she'd grabbed the door to pull it open. It cost a nigga a buck-twenty three times a week to keep the chariot washed and waxed. Keepin' my temper in check I resisted the urge to point that shit out and headed for the closest IHOP. You know how a nigga do, fuck, eat, and sleep.

# B-side

## 2

He never ceased to amaze me. Pissed, I slammed my BlackBerry down on the counter and immediately regretted the action. My insurance wasn't going to cover me for another replacement phone. Rasheed's temper had been the reason I'd replaced the last two after he crushed one under the car tire and threw another out of our front door. I rotated the phone between my French-manicured hands, inspecting the screen to make sure I hadn't added another nick or ding to the metallic pink casing. I could feel myself getting worked up. Rasheed knew I had to be at work in four hours, he knew I had contracts to review, clients to meet, and a shitload of housework on top of all that. All I ever asked was that the nigga come home when he said he would.

Trey moaned and tossed on the couch in the living room. I walked over and placed my cheek against his forehead, feeling a little bit of relief. He wasn't as hot as he'd felt earlier; maybe his fever was finally breaking. Bad enough I had to leave work early to pick him up from daycare, so I couldn't afford not to go in in the morning. He hadn't been keeping food down at all and the daycare was certain it was a flu virus. Those daycare heffas were so quick to diagnose a child and send him home. But for all I knew my baby really could have the flu, and you would think his daddy would be a little more concerned. I hefted Trey up into my arms and carried him into his bedroom. My baby was getting so tall and lanky, big for a two-year-old. My cell rang from the other room just as I'd tucked the cover under his chin.

"Damn. Chelly, you watchin' this shit on TV? They runnin' a *Snapped* marathon an' this mufukin' bitch killed erebody!" Larissa was talking a mile a minute, leaving me no room to respond. "Girl, her ass was free fo' damn near ten years befo' they caught her! Fuck, she took the nigga money, sold the house—"

"Hi, Ris, I'm good. How are you and how did you know I was still awake?" That's how you had to do when Larissa was on one of her tirades. If I didn't interrupt she'd give me the rundown of the whole damn episode, scene by scene.

"Girl, I'm sorry. You know how my ass is when somethin' good is on. I knew you'd be up, 'cause I know you. How was your day today, sweetie?"

"Trey got sick at daycare and, as much as I didn't want to, I had no choice but to go see 'Heman-Shebitch' and tell him I needed the rest of the day off." I sighed heavily into the phone. Heman-Shebitch was the name I'd given Kenny Soloman, the regional manager of the bank I worked for and the only person hell-bent against me becoming VP of the mortgage group. He had the whole exotic mail-order wife, picture-perfect marriage, and fake-ass persona thing down pat. He was one of those identity-confused black men who simply had a hard time dealing with an intelligent and self-assured black woman. His life's purpose was to point out to the entire senior management staff the fact that I was a twenty-four-year-old unwed black woman with a child and a hood-ass baby daddy.

"Oh, hell. Not his bitch ass! Chelly, promise when you get in charge ya first order of business is gonna be to fire his whack, no-life-havin' self. He jus' mad he gotta look at yo fine ass ereday knowin' he ain' got the equipment to put it down!"

We laughed. Ris was always good at making me smile. "Um . . . so where da hell is yo' baby daddy?" You could cut the sarcasm with a knife. She knew where Rasheed was, or what I should say is that she knew where Rasheed claimed to be.

"Same as last night and the night before, Ris. He's working." I didn't sound convincing, not even to my own ears. I'd been trying to give Rasheed the benefit of the doubt, but he was making it next to impossible for me to believe he wasn't out doing dirt.

"Okay, Michelle. So that's the game we playin' right now, huh? Otha than the afta-hours spot, there ain't a damn club in Virginia that stays open past two-thirty. I say we go find his ho'n ass!"

"No, momma. It's okay. Trey's fever broke and I need to try to get some kind of sleep so I can review this contract with these clients tomorrow. I'm just tired, Ris. I'm getting so tired." My voice caught in my throat and the line beeped with an incoming call. It was Rasheed.

"Let me call you in the morning, okay?" I rushed Ris off the line, anxious to see what excuse he was calling to give me. That seemed to be my life these days. Wait for Rah to call, wait for Rah to come home, wait for Rah to fuck up so I could catch him in a lie; I was always waiting for Rasheed.

This was a far cry from the family life I grew up with. My momma came home from work every day and cooked dinner for my father, who in turn brought his ass home every day at a reasonable time so we could all sit and have a meal as a family. My parents had what I liked to consider the real American Dream. They'd been married for nearly thirty years and were still each other's best friend. As far as they knew, me and Rasheed were perfectly happy together. I couldn't bring myself to tell them I spent most of my time miserable and in doubt. I closed my eyes and silently prayed for strength. I hit the "accept incoming call" option, mentally preparing myself for another battle of the sexes.

"Yes, Rasheed?" I waited but could only hear background noise. He was talking to someone and it was hard to make out his words over the background noise. "Rasheed, hello?" No response. This nigga had actually "butt-dialed" me. Somehow his phone was in his back pocket, and since I was probably the last number in his call log, when he sat down the phone dialed my number back.

It felt wrong, almost stalker-ish to eavesdrop on his conversation, but I couldn't bring myself to press the end button. I could tell from the bumps every three or four seconds that he was driving. The radio was low and garbled and I still couldn't hear who he was talking to or what he was saying. I placed the phone on speaker and carried it with me into the bedroom as I tied up my hair and got ready for bed. I'd listened to nearly twenty minutes of garbled noise and was debating on hanging up. Silently I dared him to give me solid proof. Let me hear him working or let me hear him doing dirt, either way I'd hear it with my own ears.

I turned off the lights and laid the phone on the pillow beside me, still on speaker, and closed my eyes. Why, God, was this man putting me through this? *Every night he goes to work and he's doing Lord knows what and I sit here and wait on him to decide if, or when, he wants to come home.* Frustration was becoming a very familiar feeling these days.

I'd actually started getting used to the unidentifiable white noise when the phone was suddenly quiet. Turning off the speaker phone I turned the audio volume as far up as it'd go, and pressed the phone so hard to my ear that it started burning. I could hear Rah's voice clearly now. He was ordering food or something. My hands started shaking and I could feel my insides starting to boil. Every damn night I came home from work and, tired or not, I cooked for his ass. Chicken

Parmesan, shrimp Alfredo, blackened salmon, you name it. I couldn't believe he had the nerve to eat out somewhere knowing I was keeping a plate warm for him.

I sat up in the bed and stared blankly ahead. I couldn't help feeling as though the shadows of our darkened bedroom somehow were laughing at the fool this man was making me out to be. Narrowing my eyes, I listened even more closely to Rah as he asked someone a question. A woman answered. She sounded young. A waitress or a drive-thru chick maybe? She was laughing, saying something back to him. My blood ran cold as ice and my grip on the phone was so tight my fingers had gone numb. My heart tap-danced in my chest at a mile a minute as I listened and waited. The fabric of his pants rubbed back and forth across the speaker, indicating that he was walking. A loud thud followed, as he got into what I suspected was his car. The phone went silent as my piece of shit BlackBerry lost its signal, making me curse out loud.

I didn't bother calling Rasheed back, or fighting the tears that were slowly burning trails down my cheeks.

# Let's Get One Thing Straight

## 3

Michelle's conversation was quickly slippin' from my mind as I watched Honey cross and uncross her legs out the corner of my eye. Michelle knew damn well she wasn't going to take Trey to no damn ER for a fever. She was just trying to find a way to force me to come home on her schedule and I sure as hell ain't appreciate that bullshit. I had started heading toward Military Highway but pulled into the abandoned Cedar Grove Shopping Center and parked. I had a few things I wanted to discuss with Honey. We'd been dealin' with each other for about four months and she definitely seemed like that ride or die chick I needed on my team. I already had Michelle, but she was my business head. Don't get me wrong. Michelle was a good girl. We went to high school together. I was the bad boy and she was the pretty brain of the school. Niggas flipped out when they found out I was fucking with her.

She held me down, though, even helped a nigga move product sometimes. She wouldn't let no other nigga even get close to her after I hit that shit. We'd been together for about eight years, hell since we were both sixteen, and when she had my son, Trey, two years ago I knew I couldn't let her go. She was my one and only baby momma. It was an official done deal. Another nigga could cancel any thought of getting with that shit. She was loyal than a muthafucka to me and me only. Michelle was like Honey in a lot of ways. She was fine and would do anything I asked, or told her to. I guess she just loved me like that. As I put the car into park, I turned to Honey.

"What's up, baby? You want to do it again?" She had that eager look in her eyes. I couldn't believe she was ready again so soon.

"Naw, boo, I'ma take care of you for sho, but right now I got to talk to you about some real shit."

"What's up?" she asked.

"I'ma ask you something and don't lie to me." I was serious. If it was one thing I didn't tolerate it was a lying bitch. The last bitch who lied to me ain't looking too good right about now. I sent a few of my soldiers to teach her a lesson. Dumb broad actually laughed in their faces, so they went the extra mile and took a blade to the corners of her mouth, slicing her open from her lip to cheek. That bitch got a permanent smile now, looks like a real-life version of the Joker now. No lie.

"You love me?" I asked her. She paused for a second, like she didn't know what to say. "What's the matter, why you actin' like I just gave you a fucking SAT question or some shit?"

"It's not that, baby," she said quietly. "It's just that I don't want you to be mad at me, or leave me."

"What the hell you talkin' 'bout, girl?"

She took a deep breath. "I mean, if I tell you how I really feel, are you going to get upset and leave me? I don't want that to happen. You the best thing that's happened to me. And you the only nigga who give a shit about me."

"Look, Honey, I ain't gonna get mad at you. For real the reason I pulled over here to talk to you is 'cause I feel like we need to make this official. You been loyal to me, at least I'm hopin' so, 'cause the way you was ridin' my ass tonight kinda got a nigga wonderin'."

She laughed. "Daddy, I ain't fucking nobody else. I just wanted to make sure you was happy so you wouldn't want to go nowhere else. I took a few classes an' I even went to this sex party."

"What the fuck you mean a sex party?" I was ready to flip. *You mean to tell me the chick I been dickin' raw been going to fuckin' orgy parties?* I leaned closer to her an' could feel my hands itchin' to go 'round her neck should she give me the wrong answer.

She had the look of a wide-eyed, frightened deer and leaned back close to the window in fear. "It was one of those sex toy parties where you can buy vibrators an' oils an' stuff. I just asked them a lot of questions so I could learn some stuff, baby. I don't know that much 'bout sex. I jus' wanted to learn ways to make you happier wit' me."

It wasn't until she had given me her explanation that I realized how scared she looked. "I'm sorry baby. I ain't mean to yell at you like that. I just got scared that you was given my shit away." I was glad she hadn't said what I was thinking. My chest had felt as if it were about to cave in for a minute. "You been watching them porno tapes I got for you, too, huh?"

She flashed me her pretty smile and shook her head yes. "Yeah, an' there was a whole lot of shit I want to try. If you up for it?"

"Oh, yeah? We'll see 'bout that later. Right now, I need an answer from you. You gonna be my girl or what?" I already knew she was gonna say yes, but I wanted to cover my own ass. This way, if she fucked up or crossed any lines that shouldn't be crossed, she couldn't use the excuse that she didn't know it was like that before I whooped her ass. Far as she knew she the only one I was fuckin' wit' and she had no reason to think otherwise. The goal is to neva let your side piece know that's all she is. You get more respect, leeway, and hella more pussy when you got a bitch thinkin' she number one. Not too many women ever dare cross a nigga like me and, hopefully, it didn't have to get to that point with Honey. I really liked her and wanted things to stay the way they were. Besides, who would want to mess up such a pretty face?

"Yes," she answered. "I've been your girl since the day you picked me."

I knew from that moment that I was gonna have everything exactly how I always imagined. I had two fine-ass, loyal women who would do anything to make me happy and I knew just where to put them to work in my life. I didn't get where I was by being dumb and I did everything for a reason.

I leaned over toward Honey's seat, waited for her to meet me the rest of the way, and planted a kiss on her lips. The deal was sealed. It was kinda funny, that was the first time I had ever kissed her and I could tell that she realized the importance of it. When you jus' fuckin' someone it's almost like an unspoken rule. You don't kiss on the mouth and you damn sure don't eat her pussy. I wanted Honey to know this was something serious. I wanted her to feel like she was special.

"Let's go get something to eat, then I gotta make a stop. After that I'm gonna take you somewhere and put yo' ass to sleep." And that's exactly what I planned on doing.

I drove across the plaza to the IHOP. Both Honey and I always ordered the same thing every time we came here; I would order the steak omelet and she always ordered the French toast with two scrambled eggs and sausage. She was so simple and uncomplicated and that was what I liked about her. Real easygoing, no stress.

Once we got inside, I decided that I didn't want to stay. I wanted to hurry and get to a place where I could relax and enjoy my time with her, no interruptions. I had to call and check on my son, and my phone had been blowin' up so I had to get back in touch with my soldiers to see how business was going.

"Honey, order my usual and get whatever you want. I need to go handle some biz, okay?" I handed her a fifty and winked, knowin' I wouldn't be gettin' any change back.

"Okay, daddy, I'll be out in a minute."

I had a few calls to make and I didn't need an audience. I walked outside and couldn't help admiring my white Lexus LFA coupe with all-white interior. I hand selected everything on her from the trim to the color of the damn thread holding the leather together. I called her Becky, my white girl. Michelle hated the car. She said it drew too much attention and was too flashy. Hell, that and the fact that I was the only nigga in all of Virginia with one made me like it even more. I climbed in and let the crisp new car and clean leather scent surround me. After pressing the start engine button on the dash I pulled my phone out of my back pocket. Bullshit-ass touch screen was locked up displaying Michelle's name and number from when I'd spoken to her earlier. I turned it off and back on again and decided to dial Michelle's number first. *Might as well get it over with.*

"What, Rasheed?" I was getting used to that tone. She was pissed and would go through hell or high water to make sure I knew it.

"Man, don't start that shit. What's going on wit' my son?" Damn, I didn't feel like going through this shit right now.

"Oh, now you care. I called you over an hour ago and told you he had a fever. I'm glad you found the time to fit us in. He's fine."

I could tell she was frustrated. I had been spending a lot of time away from her. Business had started to pick up all of a sudden. I had acquired a few high-paying clients who were always in need of some product. They were some big-name people so I decided to handle those clients personally, which sometimes had me hanging out at some late-night and overnight parties.

"Baby, don't act like that." I tried to calm her down a little bit. "I know I been gone but you know what I been doing. How that mortgage going to get paid if I ain't handling my shit? Come on now."

"Whatever, Rasheed."

That was her favorite response. I acted like I didn't even hear her. "You miss me? I miss you too. I mean, I ain't going to lie, I probably won't be home tonight 'cause I still have a bunch of runs to make, but I promise I'll be there when you an' li'l man get home tomorrow." I was hoping that would be enough to make her feel better.

"Damn, Rasheed, I gotta wait until six o'clock tomorrow to see my own damn man. If you ask me, your little flunkies you out buyin' late-night snacks and shit for is your damn girl! They get more time with you than me or your son. I can't believe you would have the nerve to take some bitch out to eat when I'm telling you Trey is sick. Fuck you." She hung up the phone.

Damn she made me mad sometimes. How the hell did she even know I'd stopped to get food? *Fuck!* My phone must have dialed out while it was in my pocket. She couldn't have heard that much, or I doubted she would have been as civil as she jus' was. I mean, shit, I paid the mortgage, groceries, and her fucking car note. The bitch didn't wear nothing cheap and neither did my son, but that wasn't enough for her. I was good to her dumb ass. She was a mortgage specialist for a large bank and I didn't ever ask her to spend a dime of her fuckin' money.

When we graduated high school and she wanted to go to expensive-ass Hampton University she didn't even have to ask; I paid for that shit no questions asked. I didn't even know what the hell she did with her money, but I knew she didn't have to spend any of it to live. I took care of all of that and whatever extra. All I wanted from her was to sit back, keep her fuckin' mouth shut, and just chill. She knew I always came through eventually. She was probably horny. You know how women get when they ain't had none. Either they find someone else to take care of that or they get real bitchy. I knew Michelle wasn't dumb enough to run out on me so she ain't have no other choice but to be a bitch right now. I decided to call her back and try to calm her down one last time.

"What, Rasheed?" I could hear her voice trembling.

"Baby, you crying? Why the hell you crying?" I asked, thinkin', *damn women are emotional. They get mad and scream like they gonna kill somebody one minute and then cry like a damn baby the next.*

"Rasheed, you leave me and Trey here alone all the time. You don't know what it's like to be lonely, to be in that bed by myself every night. To have your son asking for his father and I can't tell him why you aren't here with him, or tell him why you aren't answering the phone or calling him back. I can't invite my friends over 'cause I never know when you and your crew are coming through to take care of some business or count money. What am I supposed to do?" she cried into the phone.

"He's two, Michelle. If he ever asks for me you tell him I'm at work. Not that he'd understand but, damn. It's not like I'm locked up or not doin' my duties as a father. No one ever said you can't have friends come over. You killin' me wit' this shit!"

I honestly didn't like hearing her like this. I had to figure something out. The last thing I needed was her breaking down and doing something drastic. She knew too much of my business, from my suppliers down to a majority of the brothas who worked the streets for me. I needed her to be on my side.

"Michelle, calm down, I'ma come through there in a minute to see about you and Trey. Then I have to go after that. I gotta get this money, baby. All right? Stop crying. I'll be there in a minute." I hung up the phone.

I looked at Honey sitting patiently inside the IHOP, waiting for our meals. She was a good girl. I knew she wouldn't ask me any questions. I would take her with me to Michelle's and tell her I gotta take care of something for a minute. I wouldn't try this shit wit' too many chicks but I was certain if I told Honey to stay put she'd do just that. Afterward, we could head to the hotel and relax for the rest of the night.

I figured that I had a few more minutes before Honey would be back so I decided to return a couple more phone calls. My boy Derrick had called while I was at the club so I decided to call him back first More than likely, he would know what all the other phone calls were about. Really, everybody was supposed to report to Derrick first, and only if they couldn't get in touch with him and if it was important, they called me. Shit, matter of fact, half the niggas I had working for me had never met me, let alone had my damn number. I dialed Derrick's number.

"What up, nig? Why y'all blowin' up my phone? "

"Yo, man, that bitch you used to fuck wit' got picked up earlier tonight. And yo, one of our niggas told us that they heard she 'bout to go down for some hard shit. You think she might flip on you? You know that bitch can't be trusted. We thinking she might try to give some info on you to reduce her sentence or to get off altogether. We just trying to handle this before it's too late, but we gotta get the word from you first."

"C'mon, D. I need more details than that. Who the hell you talkin' 'bout?" A thousand and one faces, some wit' names an' many without, flashed across my mind.

"Damn, dawg. It's like that? Rah, I'ma need you to start keepin' a logbook! It's Danita, nigga. She let some nigga she was fuckin' set up a hydro lab in her damn garage. DEA caught wind an' raided the house. Old boy let Danita catch the case."

I had met this young hood rat way before I started fucking with Honey. Me and Michelle were on one of our "off-seasons." That's when she got pissed 'bout somethin' and no matter what I said, accordin' to her I was lyin' or bullshittin', so we ended up splittin' up for a few months. Well that was one of our longer separations and a nigga needed some company. I jus' had a hard time lettin' Danita go when Michelle wanted to be "on" again. Everything seemed cool at first, but after dealin' wit' Danita for a few months I started noticin' li'l shit. I'd go over to her place wit' two or three Gs in my money clip and be missin' a few hundred when I'd go out the nex' day. I'd started gettin' suspicious, and she proved me right when I caught her ass plottin' to rob me after count one night. She was just an ungrateful-type broad. I was breaking her off decent. I mean, the bitch lived in the projects and didn't work no-damn-where. I even bought the ho a car. She ain't appreciate none of that. Had to be greedy and try to get more. I took care of that, though. Yeah, her ass was lookin' jus' like the damn Joker now.

I wasn't worried about her telling anything. I thought she figured out from the last incident that if she fucked with us again it would be more than just her face that would be taken away. I was gonna make sure I left her place with her life.

"Naw, Derrick," I said, "Just keep ya ear to the ground and put the word out to the rest of them niggas that she locked up. Spread the word at County that if anyone hears anything about us from her mouth to get back to us and we got something for 'em." I was pretty confident that she wouldn't be an issue, but just in case.

"All right, man, I got you. We on that shit. Oh, yeah, don't forget we got count tomorrow at four. I'll make sure to call all them li'l niggas to remind them 'cause you know they lame asses don't keep up wit' that shit."

"Yeah," I answered. I knew one thing, though; they better have that money right or it was gonna be some shit. That was one reason I hated fuckin' with them young niggas, but they had to learn the biz at some point and they were cheap labor. They were just like young broads. You could throw them a few dollars and they thought they had something. Shit, half of them still lived at home. As long as they had some money to give to they moms and some money left over to go shopping and show off to the young hoes, they was straight. Just as I had hung up with Derrick, Honey walked up to the car.

"I got you some steak sauce, baby," she said as she sat down in the car. She was so thoughtful. I had forgot all about my steak sauce and I woulda been pissed when we got to the hotel 'cause I couldn't eat that shit without it.

"That's what's up." That was my way of telling her thank you.

"Look, I gotta make a stop before we head to the hotel, all right? You can go ahead and eat in the car 'cause it's probably gonna take a minute. Just be careful an' don't worry about mine. I'll just heat that shit up when we get to where we going."

"Damn, I must really be special if you gonna let me eat in here." She giggled and shuffled her food out of the bag.

"Whateva. You jus' make sure you don't drop a fuckin' crumb an' we cool." I couldn't help bein' anal 'bout certain things. When a nigga finally get some nice shit it be the dumbasses who ain't neva had nothin' to be the first ones to fuck it up.

As I drove the ten minutes to Michelle's I found myself glancing over at Honey. She just ate her food quietly and never asked me anything more than what I told her. I figured that she must really trust me and that's what I needed from her. Whether I deserved it or not I needed that from a woman: unquestionable trust.

# Another Love TKO

## 4

"Ooh, baby. Whose house is this?" Honey stared eagerly at the one-story brick home that I shared with Michelle and Trey. From the outside it looked elegantly massive with the chandelier glowing through the arched window high above the double French front doors.

"This my homeboy crib. He locked up an' I promised to help his wife wit' shit while he gone. I came over earlier to check their water heater an' I forgot to leave her some cash to pay the plumber so they can replace it tomorrow. I'ma jus' run in for a sec okay?" I kissed Honey on the forehead. "Since you been such a good student I'ma need you to use that imagination an' show me at least three new positions when we get to the room." I leaned over and reclined her seat just a bit. I left Honey concentratin' on what we would do later and made my way up to the house. I tried to think of how I could keep Michelle occupied and away from the window. Before I could even finish turning my key in the lock I could hear my son knocking on the other side of the door screaming, "Daddy." I loved to hear him call my name.

Michelle peeked around the barely opened door; I nudged it just wide enough to slide in. I could see the red in her eyes from her crying. I didn't even say anything to her; I just grabbed her around her waist and kissed her. I walked a little farther inside and shut the door behind me. As I kissed her, I could feel all of her tension seep out and her body went limp. I would have probably taken her right there if it weren't for my son tugging on my leg. I released her lips and bent down to pick up my son. I couldn't believe he was still up at this hour.

"Hey, man, what are you doing still up?" His only response was to call my name as he laid his head on my shoulder. Damn, he did feel a li'l warm. I guessed Chelle was tellin' the truth. I walked into the living room and sat on the couch with my family. My woman by my side, my son on my lap. It felt good to be there with them. I guessed it didn't dawn on me how much I missed them until I was back with them and saw their faces. Michelle looked fine as hell no matter what time of day it was. Even now with her hair pulled back in a ponytail and her pajamas on, she was fine.

We didn't say anything to each other; we just sat there like we did sometimes and enjoyed feeling each other's presence. Her head rested on my shoulder opposite Trey's and her hand tangled with mine. Before I knew it, my son had fallen asleep in my arms. I got up to put him in his room. I placed him in his bed and kissed him on his forehead.

He was my future. I never had my father and I was going to make sure that he never had to grow up like I did. I was going to make sure I was there for him and that he would be left with something besides my name when I left this place. It was becoming clearer to me each day that I wanted to see Trey grow up. I wanted to be there when he graduated high school, bought his first car, asked me for girl advice for the first time. I needed to get some paper stacked up so I could finally go legit.

I turned to leave and saw Michelle standing in the doorway watching me. Even in the dark, she was beautiful. She always reminded me of this china doll I'd seen at my aunt's when I was a kid. Huge, luminous hazel eyes surrounded by thick, dark lashes sittin' in a heart-shaped face. The way the light from the hallway shined around her made her look just like an angel.

"Come here, baby," I told her. She walked over to me kind of slow, like she wasn't sure if she should come or not. I hugged her and whispered, "I'm so sorry I wasn't here when you needed me. You know I love you, Chelle."

She timidly pulled away from me and stepped out into the hallway.

"Show me you love me, Rasheed."

I knew what she wanted. She wanted me to make love to her. But I couldn't. I still had Honey in the car waiting for me and I had already promised her another ass waxing. I decided that I had to do the next best thing that would satisfy her and make sure I didn't wear myself out.

I closed Trey's door behind me and grabbed the back of Michelle's neck, pulling her to me. I kissed her long and hard and continued until I could hear her breathing heavily. I slowly slid her down to the carpeted floor and began to move from her lips to her neck, and stayed there until her hands moved from her side to the back of my head.

"God, Rasheed," she whispered, "why do you do this to me?"

I didn't answer. She didn't want an answer. She just wanted me to continue to make her feel good and I knew exactly how to do that. I lifted her shirt up, exposing her breasts. I grabbed one in each hand and began to kiss and suck on them one at a time. She slowly let out a sigh and slid her hand down to the crotch of my pants. I knew I had to move quickly or else I would be in a position I couldn't get out of.

I sat up and began to pull her pants down slowly. As I did, I trailed kisses down the soft, warm skin of her stomach, past her navel, and stopped when I got to my destination. I was going to make sure she slept well tonight. I kissed her slowly on her moistened lips, letting her get used to the sensation before I parted her folds with my tongue and gave her what she had been waiting for. I used my tongue to cover every inch of her peach. I took turns licking and sucking and took enjoyment in hearing her moan and feeling her arch her back. I grabbed her waist and held her tightly, making sure she didn't get away from me.

She repeatedly called my name and told me over and over how much she loved me. All of this just made my head even bigger. When I thought she was getting close to that point I stuck two fingers inside of her as I flicked my tongue over her clit, and began to stroke her as if it were me inside. She lost control and I had to place my hand over her mouth. It was like there was so much passion inside that she had to let it out. She began licking the underside of my hand as I fucked her with my fingers and my tongue.

Finally, she squeezed her legs together tightly and let out a sound of pure ecstasy.

My work was done. I slowly slid my fingers from inside her and sat up. I couldn't front, a nigga's mouth was tired and I was glad she finally got hers. She pulled me to her and kissed her juices from my mouth. I knew she was content.

"Baby, I have to get ready to go. I gotta go ahead and take care of this business so you can have me all to yourself tomorrow."

"Okay, Rasheed," she said, barely able to breathe. "I love you."

"I love you too," I said, and I meant it.

I helped her up off the floor and she began to fix her clothes. I headed toward the front door but decided to stop at the bathroom before heading out. That's all I needed was to get in the car with pussy all on my lips and chin. I already had one broad asking questions, I didn't need two. I took a quick piss; my shit was a little hard so it took a minute. Then I washed my hands real good like them doctors be doing. Shit, you woulda thought a nigga was about to go into surgery. I was scrubbing like hell. I scrubbed my mouth the same way and gargled with the mouthwash underneath the sink.

I kissed Michelle on the cheek and told her to lock the door. She kissed me one more time and I closed the door behind me. When I got into the car, Honey had reclined the seat back and was fast asleep. Good, no questions, and it gave me a chance to catch my breath. I started the car and headed for the hotel. I was definitely gonna have to eat and take a nap before I did anything else tonight.

# And Still Counting

## 5

I jumped up from the bed, startled by something. I wasn't sure what it was. I also wasn't sure where the hell I was. I turned to my left and saw Honey's sandy brown hair peeking from underneath the covers, and then I remembered. We were at the hotel. That's what happens when you try to be the shit and knock off two chicks in one night.

I looked at the alarm clock on the hotel nightstand. It was 6:00 A.M. Damn, a nigga's day was starting already. I had to meet up with the crew around 4:00 P.M. to do count. I always got there a few hours early. I drove around a few times first to make sure things looked normal and calm. If one thing looked out of place I would call the count off or switch up our spot.

I really ain't feel like going through all that extra precautious shit today, but I definitely didn't mind since paper in my pocket was the end re-sult. We did count about twice a week depending on how fast shit was selling. Last week we had to do count three times. That was a first. But you ain't see this nigga complaining.

I always walked out of count wit' no less than ten Gs. So that was thirty Gs last week and this being our second count for this week, which was another twenty. That ain't even including the money I got from my political connects. Virginia is stupid strict when it comes to strip clubs and black owners. It's almost like they find reasons to shut down black-owned establishments just for the hell of it. I had a few politicians who came in here and there. Old, stuffy, straight-as-an-arrow-lookin' white muthafuckas. They got a couple of dances for free, the girls offered a little hot mouth, and since Martha or Ingrid ain't put-tin' it down at home, they accepted. In return I got a li'l extra pocket money and my spot stayed official. I wouldn't have been surprised if we had another three-count week before the month was over with.

I was starting to get too much money. I didn't know what to do with it. It ain't smart to leave that shit where you lay your head and I definitely didn't want to put it in a bank. If a nigga get caught up that's the first place the Feds look. I wanted to make sure that if something did happen to me my son would still have something left. Michelle had helped me get some real estate with most of the money so my shit seemed legit. I already owned three apartment complexes, an office building with ten suites, a condo complex with six units, and I was partial owner of the Hot Spot.

That's where we did our counts. It was like our little hangout. I picked the basement of the Hot Spot for our counts for one simple reason: after count, most of the crew ended up upstairs with the dancers, spendin' the money they just got on some money-hungry ho, when they had families at home they needed to be taking that money to. But shit, that just put my money back into my pocket.

The way me and my boy Derrick ran the club was a sure-fire guarantee that we made cake. We charged the dancers who lap danced a booth rental fee, just like them hair salons. In return they got their own private station that they could have set up any way they wanted. We even let them choose their own lighting. I got the idea from a movie I was watchin' and all these Broadway bitches had their own little makeup mirrors and dressing station's setup. I figured strippers are damn close to actresses, might as well let them have their own space. My homeboy worked for this business that set up office cubicles anywhere. One of our areas was nothing but a row of cubicle walls without the desks. Some bitches had love seats, others had recliners and shag rugs.

It kinda helped with business 'cause it made our customers feel like they could be more discreet. They didn't have to worry about other clients watching them cum on themselves. And the ladies felt more in control. Having their own station made them feel like the client was coming into their territory. I thought it made them perform better. They fixed it up so they felt comfortable. Shit, I say whatever make the money come in was what the fuck we were gonna keep doin'.

We also offered safes in each booth so that the girls had somewhere to put their money besides the dressing room. This way, we didn't have to worry about girls stealin' and the scheming-ass hoes couldn't lie and say they had their shit stolen to try to get out of paying their fees. Only three people knew the codes to the safes and that was the dancer, Derrick, and me. It seemed to be working so far. Still, I wanted to get the count over with.

Honey began to move around in the bed. It dawned on me that I never did hit her off that second time. Shit, my ass was tired last night. But I figured I was rested up enough for a quickie.

"Wake up, sexy." She began to stretch and turned over to me with a smile.

"Why you up so early, daddy?"

"You'll see. Turn back over, I owe you one, remember?" I wanted to get right to it, without using up all my energy.

I ordered a Heineken from Annette, the bartender. I didn't want to drink too heavily during count. When you get fucked up, your money can end up fucked up too. Besides, I had to see Michelle and Trey later on today. I didn't want to be around them liquored up.

I saw most of the crew's cars in the parking lot, so I knew we could go ahead and get started when I got downstairs. I wanted to check out our surveillance cameras first, though. No one knew about the cameras but me. I had one hidden camera on the bar with a view of the cash register (bartenders steal too), one in each booth (that way I knew who was fucking or giving blowjobs for extra dough), one each on the front and back doors, and one in the count room in the basement. Everyone in the crew had access to the count room at any time, so I wanted to keep an eye on whoever thought they were able to do something in secret there. That's how I'd caught Danita plotting to steal from me.

It was only 2:30 P.M. so I had a little bit 'til it was time to start. Plus, I knew them niggas. They were having a good time drinking and feelin' up on the hoes. That would keep 'em busy for a minute. My office was like my second home. I sat behind my desk and entered my password into my desktop, opening my "eye in the sky" archive. I fast-forwarded through most of the first day. The room was empty the whole day except for Day Day from the crew and Ecstasy, one of the strippers, sneaking off to fuck. I had to laugh when I saw that shit 'cause the clip didn't even last five minutes. Quick-ass motherfucker! If it weren't for the fact that I didn't want anyone knowing about the camera, I would've been jokin' the hell out his ass.

Video two surprised me a little. I saw Diamond, one of my top earners, and myself walk into the room. I stopped the footage and then changed my mind and pressed play. I wanted to see it again in real time. I saw myself sit down in a chair at the table. Diamond walked over and I placed a bill in her hand. I remember giving her a hundred dollar bill. I already knew what she was working with and it was damn sure worth it.

Diamond was a bad bitch and I probably woulda made her mine, but I had her on surveillance down here with too many niggas in my crew. I even had her on tape in her booth fucking just about everything that came through it, even a few of the dikes who frequented the club. She was too loose for me but that pussy was good as shit, not to mention the dome piece.

I watched as she sucked my dick then placed a condom on and backed up on it. I was enjoying it more from this view. I was able to see her calf muscles flex as she moved herself up and down on my dick. I could watch the expressions on her face and as I did, I relived every feeling I had during our escapade. I turned off the tape. The last thing I needed was to go to the meeting with my shit sticking out. I would watch it again later. I made my way back out into the bar area.

"What up, nigga?" Big Baby sauntered in through the door to my office. This nigga had the laziest laid-back stride. I didn't think I'd ever seen his big ass move in a hurry for any-thing. "Glacial paces" was what I called that shit. Watchin' that nigga walk was like watchin' an ice glacier make its way across the ocean. Slow.

"Nothin', nigga, I know one thing though, y'all niggas had better have my money." I minimized the surveillance footage just in case he glanced toward my screen.

"Oh, for sho nigga. You know I been on my crew hard 'cause I want my damn cut. I got appointments and thangs once dis shit over wit'. Jingling dingling, nigga!"

Big Baby was a funny dude. If you couldn't tell from his name, Big Baby was a big dude and he had a baby face. He looked just like a little kid in a grown-ass man's body. Most of his appointments probably wouldn't even be fucking with his ass if it weren't for his humor and his money. He walked over and handed me a small, crumpled piece of paper.

"You said you wanted all the VIP drops to come to you personally. This one is big, it's for this afternoon. You want me to roll wi'chu on it?" I looked down at Big Baby's chicken scratch on the back of an old Pizza Hut receipt. I was very familiar with the number. I needed no help handlin' this one.

"Nah, my nig, I got it. How 'bout you go invest in some Post-it notes or somethin', nigga, and stop eatin' so much fuckin' Pizza Hut. C'mon let's get this count out the damn way." Big Baby's arm felt like it weighed a solid ton as he dropped it roun' my shoulder. I couldn't imagine how the hell any woman survived after a night underneath his oversized ass.

"Let's do dis then," he said, and we both headed down the stairs and entered the room to start the count.

"'Bout damn time, nigga. Shit, I done told you when we got business, pull the dick out yo' mouth." I ain't even have to look in the direction of the voice 'cause I already knew Derrick's smart-ass mouth.

"Nigga, fuck you, I was watchin' yo' moms suckin' my pops," I threw back.

"Yeah, well you know my moms is good like that. She learned from yo' moms." Derrick never missed a beat. With this fool we could go back and forth all night.

"Whateva, man. Let's get this fuckin' money 'cause I owe yo' sister for last night." The room broke out in laughter. We liked to keep the atmosphere light and relaxed, but we all knew it was serious business. Derrick stood up from his chair in the corner and took a seat at the head of the table. I let him run the count and together we counted the end results. He began to call each of the crew members one by one to bring their money and have their cut counted out and given to them. Everything was looking good. We were going to be able to get everything situated and I could get outta here and take care of Michelle and Trey.

As I looked around the room, mentally doing a head count, I realized that someone was missing. I hadn't seen Shy Money come or leave. I wasn't going to interrupt the count but I made a mental note to ask Derrick if he knew what was up. I knew something wasn't right. And, damn it, that meant my money wasn't going to be right. Derrick was doing the last crew member's count. Most of them had already headed upstairs. Big Baby was the first one to leave. I figured he had plans with one of the strippers. As the last person left, I approached Derrick.

"Yo, nigga, where Shy Money? He ain't even show up today. You heard from him?" I was hot. I knew that if I didn't know anything Derrick better had or somebody was in some shit.

"Yeah, man, I was waiting for everybody to kick rocks before I talked to you about that. Nigga, Shy got pinched." He said it with some hesitation.

"What the hell happened? Did he have anything on him?" I was a little concerned myself. If he had some product on him, it opened a whole lot of doors I wasn't ready to try to close.

"Naw, his girl called me earlier," Derrick explained. "She said they were on the way to the store when a cop pulled them over. She said Shy's license wasn't good. This his umpteenth time gettin' caught drivin' an' his shit suspended.

Stupid fuck. He ain't have shit on him, but he had all the money for the count in the glove compartment."

"Damn, why didn't Keisha get it and bring it to you?"

"Yeah, that would be easy if she had it. She said the cop was an ass, made them get out and searched the car. She said after they found the money, they made her get her purse, took Shy to jail, and called a tow to impound the car."

Regardless of him being locked up, he owed me that paper no matter what. He would have to hustle extra hard or take a loan out to repay me the paper the cops confiscated, or I'd have to take his life. You can't cut nobody slack in this game. Kindness is always taken as weakness, so you treat ere nigga like they ain't shit. If I let one nigga slide and the rest of 'em caught wind, I'd have ended up gettin' tried by ere nigga in the camp.

"Damn, which cop was it? He ain't on payroll?" I had Norfolk police on lock but if it was a Virginia Beach bitch that shit was as good as gone.

"Nah, Keisha said they were out Bayside and she had to walk back home 'cause she ain't have shit on her, no cell phone, no money, not even some change for the payphone. You know she's pregnant, too."

"So I take it that nigga still locked up?" Shy spent his money like water. He never had anything left between counts. I knew Keisha couldn't bail him out. I didn't know what he be doing with his money but he should have been gettin' his license straight.

"Look D, I gotta meet Michelle and li'l man at the crib in a few. Call Jerry and arrange to get the fool out. Once you pick him up, make sure you let him know that he is going to have to put in some extra work to get that shit back. Call me when you done so we can figure out how we gonna fix this shit."

I knew Derrick would handle his business. Jerry, our bail bondsman, was on the books so we ain't even have to worry about actually puttin' some shit down. Jerry got a li'l something every month whether one of ours had been locked up or not. That way, if it happened, we were already taken care of, no matter how many were locked up at a time.

"Yeah, Rah, I'll holla at you later tonight. Make sure you fuck Michelle real good for me."

I didn't even bother to respond. We all knew that would never happen. That was my nigga, though. We had been friends for so long I knew that joking with me like that was his way of saying he loved me. That was my brother. Most of the dudes in my crew were like li'l brothers to me. Regardless of that, though, they knew they had better have my money, and Shy was fuckin' up.

# Miss-taken Identity

# 6

Michelle hadn't gotten home yet so I decided to try to be a li'l romantic. I hadn't done anything nice for her in a minute, so I had to think of something that would stick in her mind for a long time in case I had to be away for a minute. I grabbed the phonebook to look through the restaurant section. As I flipped the pages, I started to think about Honey. I left her at the hotel earlier and told her I had paid for two more days. I arranged for Derrick to pick her up and take her to work and bring her back. She was staying with her cousin, who was a crackhead and always had a bunch of strangers running in and out of her house. Honey couldn't stand being there so, occasionally, I paid for a hotel room for her for a few days, sometimes a week.

She had only been working at the Hot Spot for six months. She made good money, but livin' with a crackhead made it hard to keep any. She was giving her cousin $600 a month, which was ridiculous 'cause the bitch was on Section 8 and her rent wasn't nothing but like $150 a month. Basically, Honey was supporting her cousin's drug habit. She wanted to buy a car but wanted to pay cash for it. I supported her with that; since we been fuckin' around I would pay for the li'l shit she needed so she could save up. I decided to call her, just to check on her and to make sure her ass was there.

"Hey, Angie, it's Rasheed. Give me room 145."

"Hey, Rasheed," Angie said.

I knew pretty much everyone who worked there. I had even made a loan to the owners a few months back. It's all business, baby, all business.

"She ain't in the room. She down here at the snack machine. I'll get her, hold on."

I could hear her put the phone down and call Honey's name.

"Who is it?" Honey asked

"Yo' future baby daddy," Angie laughed in response.

"Hey, baby, you checkin' up on me?"

I could hear the smile in her voice. I knew she liked it when I called her out of the blue like that. It made her feel special or important, like I was thinking about her, which I was.

"You know it. What you gettin' out the snack machine? Yo' ass already thick enough, don't overdo it. You gonna be on stage tryin' to drop it and drop through the floor. I'ma make you pay for the repairs."

"Shut up, crazy," she said as she laughed. "I just got tired of being in the room. Are you coming through tonight?"

"Naw, boo. I got some shit to take care of. You just make sure you make that money tonight 'cause yo' ass definitely need a car. A nigga get tired of drivin' yo' ass everywhere. When you gonna drive me around?" I liked fuckin' with her. I couldn't mess with Michelle like that. She was too sensitive.

"As soon as you give me the keys to yo' Lex, nigga!"

"Hell, naw. Never mind then. I'ma holla at you before the night is over wit'. Derrick should be there to get you in a minute."

"All right. Bye, baby." She hung up the phone.

I had come across a restaurant that I thought Michelle would like. I had meetings there a few times with the mayor but I had never taken Michelle there. It was a nice, classy restaurant called Rockefeller's. The food was expensive but very good. There were candles on every table and a white baby grand piano in the middle with a man in a tuxedo who played romantic music all night. She would love it. Shit, I was even impressed when I first went. They have this big-ass water fountain made of white stucco in front with lights shining on it that changed from pink to orange to blue. The building itself was made of white stucco as well. It kinda had that Italian/Spanish feel to it. If I was a bitch and a nigga took me to a spot like that, off top I would be givin' up the drawers! I knew she wouldn't forget tonight if I took her there.

I called my mom and asked her to keep Trey for the night. I knew she wouldn't mind 'cause we hadn't been over to see her in a couple of weeks. Plus, I always broke her off a li'l something when I saw her and she was satisfied, even if it meant she had to miss her Bingo night with her girlfriends. Just as I hung up, Michelle walked through the door. As soon as Trey saw me, he began to squirm in her arms to get down. She let him go and he took off in my direction.

"Hey, man." I took him up into my arms; he didn't say a word. He just put his head on my shoulder and continued to suck his pacifier.

"He's tired," Michelle said. "The daycare worker said he wouldn't take a nap today. He must have known you were gonna be home today. He's been all excited and wouldn't keep still since I picked him up." She walked over and kissed me. I enjoyed it. But it made me start thinking about shit I didn't like thinking about. I loved Michelle and my son. I knew they deserved someone to be there with them all the time. I also knew that Michelle deserved someone who would be consistent and faithful to her, but I just wasn't that nigga. I didn't even think I would feel right. It's like having that freedom helps me feel in control. I needed that more than anything.

"I got a surprise for you," I told her.

"Oh yeah, what is it? Did you buy me something? I hope it ain't no clothes 'cause you always be picking out that hoochie-lookin' stuff and you know I don't dress like that." Michelle was always in pantsuits or business skirts. I understood her job be on that professional shit, but damn. For once I'd have liked to see her in a damn miniskirt or somethin' that fit skintight. Don't get me wrong, she looked damn good in that schoolteacher and pinned-up bun kinda way, but sometimes I just wanted to see her let all that shit go. I was workin' with all these bitches all day who just let it hang out, and it's whack to come home to the same old bland shit every damn day.

"Naw, I get tired of yo' ass takin' shit back. You don't even have the decency to wear the shit once just to satisfy me. I ain't buying you no more damn clothes. We goin' out."

"I hope it ain't a club 'cause you know I've gotta work in the morning. I can't stay up all night and then get back up like you."

She made me sick sometimes. She couldn't just keep quiet and just listen to what I had to say before she started assuming and complaining. I was trying to do something nice for her but she was gonna make me change my mind before she even found out what the surprise was.

"Shut up, Michelle, damn. I'm taking you to Rockefeller's." She shut up all right. She let out a squeal, jumped up, and put her arms around my neck.

"Oh, baby, I heard about that restaurant. It's nice. Thank you. Oh my God, what am I gonna wear? I gotta do my hair." She couldn't even think straight. She had grabbed the diaper bag and set it on top of the refrigerator. She hadn't even taken out Trey's cups. I just shook my head and laughed.

"Girl, just go upstairs and pick something out for you and me, and start on ya head 'cause I don't want to hear shit about your hair not looking right when it's time to go. I'ma put Trey down for a nap. Momma is gonna keep him so we gotta leave a little early to drop him off." I didn't even think she heard everything I said, 'cause when I turned around she was nowhere to be found.

Women. Especially that one. They were funny as hell but I loved 'em.

As we pulled into the parking lot of Rockefeller's, Michelle's eyes became as wide as fucking walnuts. I figured that tonight I would do the whole gentleman thing. I parked the car and told Michelle to stay where she was. I had to tell her what to do 'cause knowing her fast ass she would have hopped out before I had a chance to be courteous. I walked over to her door and opened it as the valet walked up to take my key. I held out my hand for her to steady herself as she got out. She was smiling. I wanted her to stay that way the rest of the evening.

"Baby," she said with a tear in her eye, "this is beautiful."

"Just make sure you relax an' enjoy yourself." I didn't want her to be uptight or upset about anything that had been goin' on over the last few weeks.

As we were taken to our table, I tipped the host. I knew how to build relationships; if I ever decided to come in here last minute or without a reservation, best believe she would remember the nigga who slipped her a hundred.

The host smiled with a slight nod and headed back to her station.

We looked over the menu and wine list as we waited for our waiter. I decided to show some interest in Michelle's day. I never really asked about her job unless I needed her to do something for me.

"How was work?" I asked her.

"Oh my God, baby, we had some crazy shit happen today," she said as she began to explain. "Somehow, someone had acquired a loan with someone else's ID and information. Apparently someone stole an ID of someone who looks similar to them, forged pay stubs for a bogus company; they even had a birth certificate and social security card for the person. Anyway, they bought this house, kept it for three months, and then sold it. It took us three months to realize that half of the paperwork was fake. Whoever it is walked away with a profit on a house that was never really theirs. It's a crazy situation."

Listening to her, I got an idea. I had been trying to figure out what to do with the extra money I didn't want to put into real estate. I didn't want to open an account in my name; too risky. But I could put it in Michelle's name.

Michelle was my girl and I loved and trusted her, but you can't let your bitch know everything. I needed to stash some money that she wouldn't know about. I could get Honey to use

Michelle's ID to open an account. Most white people thought all blacks looked alike anyway, and they would be so excited about getting Honey's money that they wouldn't really pay attention to the photo. I could get Michelle's ID and social security card tonight, then pick up Honey in the morning to open the account.

Honey would do whatever I told her. And I would make sure to be right beside her while she opened it to make sure she didn't keep any of the account information. I would have her use the address to the club for the account, that way all the bank statements would come to me. And I would keep the ATM card and checkbook. If I needed to make a large withdrawal, I could get Honey to do it. It was perfect.

The waiter had arrived to take our order. We ordered the veal with capers in an orange garlic glaze and risotto. I couldn't even tell you if the food was good. I was so excited about my plan. I wanted to eat and go to sleep so I could hurry up and get to tomorrow. I still had business to take care of and needed to get Michelle home and settled so I wouldn't catch hell when I left to take care of my VIP client.

I rushed us through the rest of the meal, anxious to get everything rolling. I'd put my phone on silent just in case Honey or anyone else decided to call. Michelle was never suspicious when it didn't ring, but if my phone rang and I ignored the call she immediately assumed I was trying to avoid talkin' to one of my side girls in front of her. And she was right.

"You haven't said a word in nearly five minutes, Rasheed. Are you okay?"

"Yeah, I had an issue earlier wit' one of my guys gettin' locked up, an' he basically left his pregnant girlfriend out in the cold 'cause he ain't put shit away." I knew if I played to her gentle nature I could get us outta here in no time.

"I promised her a small loan to handle they rent and shit until he get out. I forgot to drop it off. That shit can wait, though." I made a nonchalant nod with my head and took a sip of my drink.

"Rasheed, please don't forget to help that girl. I can't imagine what she must be going through right now." It amazes me how women can show so much concern for people they've never even met. All it takes is a piss-poor hard-luck story and they ready to be someone's savior. But Michelle wasn't foolin' me. She categorized all the women I dealt with into two categories: fuckable and not fuckable. The only reason she was gung-ho about me helpin' someone out was 'cause she obviously believed Shy's girlfriend was unfuckable, otherwise the questioning would have been worse than the Spanish Inquisition.

$245 later we were finally on our way home. Michelle happy and satisfied and me ready to get the fuck to work. We were waiting for the valet to bring our car around when Michelle caught me off guard.

"Damn, Rah, what's goin' on tonight? No phone calls from the crew, no texts. You ain't foolin' me. What you do, put your phone on silent? Who were you scared about calling you?"

It never fuckin' failed. I swore Michelle just looked for things to fight over. If my phone rang I was fuckin' up, if it didn't ring I was fuckin' up.

"Damn, Michelle! I'm tryin' to put all the bullshit aside an' spend some quality time wit' yo' ass an' you still wanna trip?"

A mild-mannered white couple had walked out of the restaurant and were watchin' us cautiously.

"You know what? I'm sorry. I think I jus' drank too much. You know I don't drink all like that."

She pouted up at me and offered her lips to me as a silent apology. I quickly pecked her back, still peeved at the expensive tab and her ungrateful-ass outburst.

"It's cool. Let's just get yo' tipsy ass home."

# The Devil Smiles in Your Face

## 7

Rasheed dropped me off at the house and barely kissed me on the cheek before flying off to handle whatever it was that had him so spaced out at dinner. That was so like him. Whenever he felt bad about something he might have done, we'd have an expensive meal or evening out and, as usual, duty would call and off he'd go. I wasn't buying his whole "Captain Save a Ho" story, but I'd forgotten that I'd made plans to have a girls' night out with Ris, and was happy we were finished and it wasn't even nine-thirty. I was pretty sure a little hot mouth on the ride home would keep him out of my hair for the rest of the night. He'd be content enough to go handle business and I could still make it out, and he'd be none the wiser.

I'd put my phone on silent at dinner just to be on the safe side. If it went off too much Rasheed would get jealous and start to question who was texting or calling me. He did so much dirt on a regular basis that it actually started to make him insecure. We'd then end up arguing and he'd stake out the house, waiting to see if anyone came or went and accuse me of cheating. Next thing you'd know I'd be out of another damn BlackBerry and he'd be using it all as an excuse to hide out at the club with his skanks. I knew his phone was on silent and I honestly didn't care, but if I didn't get him just a little riled up I couldn't guarantee that he'd drop me off and leave like he did.

I fished my phone out of my slate and black Christian Louboutin purse. You'd think a bag that cost over $3,000 would at least offer you the luxury of a cell phone slot. I'd only missed two calls from Ris. I grabbed my keys and was happy that it wasn't too hot or humid out, otherwise I'd feel the need to take another shower. I got into my car and immediately pressed the phone button.

"Call Ris. Cell." Everything was voice controlled from the radio to the navigation.

"Girl, yo' ass betta be on the fuckin' way or I'm gonna go the hell off an' I ain't playin'!"

"Hi, sweetie, I'm sorry I'm running a little behind. Trey was fussy so I had to stay and calm him down. I'm on my way right now." Larissa couldn't stand when I stood her up, or put Rah before her. In her eyes, she'd stood by me and helped me in so many ways that she trumped any situation that involved him. It definitely wouldn't help right now if she knew I was late because of his ass.

"Aww, how is my li'l punkin? Chelly, I've already started drinkin', so ya ass gonna have to play catch up!"

"Catch up my ass! Where are we going? You know I'm not drinking all like that if I'm driving."

"It's a surprise! I need to get you out from under ya mufuckin', turd-ass, no-good nigga of a baby daddy, so you can see there's more to life than dealin' wit' bullshit ereday!"

In a sense, Ris was right. How long could I go on brushing aside the lies and the deception? I'd been dealing with his bullshit so long that it really was starting to become a normal part of life for me. I was not getting any younger, and one of my biggest fears was to be stuck with more kids than I could handle and an MIA baby daddy. I honestly didn't need to have this conversation right now. I just wanted to get a little wasted and enjoy a much needed break from Rasheed and Trey.

"Ris, I'll be there in a few. Do you look like a hoochie, because I'm wearing Valentino and this shit is expensive so I'm not changing." If I gave her a heads-up on how I was dressed, then she'd have plenty of time to go switch up her outfit. Sometimes Ris got a little too carried away and her looks usually bordered on partially naked or totally hooker.

"Girl, I look damn good an' that's all ya ass needs to know. Somebody otha than me need to enjoy this muthafuckin' view!"

We laughed and I ended the call, curious as to where the hell this girl was going to have me tonight. It was always a mystery or a surprise with her. I sighed and checked my reflection in the rearview mirror. Yes, I too was looking damn good. If Rah wasn't going to appreciate all this, I needed to go be up in someone's face who would.

Ris dragged me nearly forty-five minutes across town to these huge *Lifestyles of the Rich and Famous*–looking mansions somewhere in Portsmouth. Some random music producer she knew had invited her to a pool party, and so here we were.

I stared through my windshield in awe at the massive structure in front of us and my eyes

widened at the array of candy-colored Bentleys
and Lamborghinis in the circular driveway. The
house was buzzing with activity and there was an
eclectic mixture of hood rats, video chicks, and
everything in between all over the place. I suddenly felt completely out of my element in my
designer skirt and blouse. Ris, on the other hand,
blended in perfectly with the scantily clad, too-
tight miniskirts, barely there see-through tops,
and six-inch-plus stiletto crowd.

"What's the matter, momma?" Ris was lookin'
over at me calmly; she already knew I was uncomfortable. She'd known me long enough to be
able to read the slightest changes in my mood.

"Ris, you know I'm not into this kind of stuff.
I mean look at me. I'm not even dressed right."

"Chelly, you trippin'! You look good, an' if
any of these hoes trip or act siddity, you already
know I'll bust a bitch to the white meat! Besides,
I'm gonna say I'm a singer an' you can pretend
you're my lawyer." She hit me with her "I'm a genius" smile and blew me a play kiss. I raised my
eyebrow and figured what the hell. Life wouldn't
be life without Ris.

I inched my car slowly into the driveway, amid
the luxury vehicles and, for once, I was thankful
for Rah's flamboyance. My gold Mercedes SL500
blended in perfectly with all the other high-pro-

file vehicles. I could tell Ris felt like a star pulling up in class, while a lot of the girls teetered on the edge of cute and about to bust they ass as they trotted up from hoopties parked up and down the street.

I parked and was doing my best to boost my self-confidence as I climbed out of my car.

Ris needed no esteem booster at all. She climbed out looking like a million dollars and poised herself, as if she really were some charismatic singing diva.

"What the fuck? Asshole!" All attention shifted to the street as two girls were nearly mowed down by a black BMW speeding past.

"Well, aren't we a classy bunch?" I laughed and was turning toward Ris when something caught my attention in the direction the car had sped from. Ris must have noticed at the same time I did.

"That muthafucka wouldn't have the nerve!" She'd blurted out loud the exact words I'd silently screamed in my mind. Sitting in the driveway of an adjacent mansion across the street was Rah's all-white unmistakable LFA. He was the only one in the area with one, and definitely the only one with all-white everything, from the interior to the rims. My heart sank in my chest as I saw him on the porch hugging, even from this distance, who appeared to be an obviously beautiful Spanish woman. The image seared itself into my brain and I took in all the details from the package in his hands to the overly friendly way she beckoned for him to come inside. I could see why he was obviously in such a rush to get dinner over with.

He was too excited to get to "work."

# All in a Day's Work

## 8

I'd never minded makin' a delivery to Solana.
Her and her husband were my favorite clients.
Solana was a hot-tempered Latina, who didn't
take shit off no one, and had to be one of the
sexiest olive-skinned, blue-eyed women I'd ever
seen in my life. The first time we all met, I was
actually more intimidated than a mufucka. I'd
gotten a call for a big delivery and was immediately suspicious. The DEA'll try all kindsa shit to
get a nigga caught up out here, and them livin' in
the middle of rich white suburbia ain't have me
too thrilled, either.

I remember pullin' up and seein' this short,
stocky monster of a Mexican mufucka wit' a neck
thicker than my thigh and arms the size of tree
trunks. He was known only as Miho, Solana's
husband, and a professional stuntman. The two
of them liked to party, and by party I mean do a

helluva lot of coke and smoke weed. Hell, we all got bills to pay. I liked to consider myself a supply manager and that jus' happened to be how I paid mine.

I made the trip across town in record time, stoppin' by my high rise along the way to pick up a key of my finest powder. The normal shit went for roughly thirty Gs a key, but this was Primo, purest shit on the market. It was an easy $60,000. I pulled up to the gate jus' as an all-black BMW 745i with pitch-black limo dark tint was pullin' out. The car slowed to a stop beside mine, blarin' salsa music loud enough to be heard outside the car. The odors of weed and heavy aftershave hit me square in the face as the window rolled down revealing Miho, cheesin' at me like a damn kid at Christmas from behind a pair of dark Gucci shades.

"Hey, *vato!* You bring that thing for my baby? She's inside, go in!" He insisted on yellin' over the damn music rather than turnin' that shit down, but that was Miho for you. Loud, obnoxious, and simply not givin' a fuck.

"Hey, from the smella thangs I need to be rollin' with chu, partna! I thought I told ya easy wit' the aftershave, one splash is enough, nigga! Damn!"

"Oh no, hombre. It's hater repellent, so chu must be a hater! And chu already know chu can't ride wit' me. Black people are cop magnets!"

Gravel flew in all directions as he sped past me, laughin' out the window before I could get back at his ass. I drove up and parked in the courtyard right in front of the house. I'd concealed the coke in a white cake box. Grabbin' the cake box out of my trunk, I made my way up the massive front steps and rang the doorbell.

You know how everyone's house got a smell. Like if people cook a lotta jasmine rice or shit with garlic it just stays in the air. I could never put my finger on it, but piña colada and somethin' else came to mind whenever I came over. I was about to ring the doorbell when the huge door swung open. Wrapped in a bright gold thigh-length leopard-print robe, Solana posed for me in the doorway like a 1950s pinup girl. Her thick, dark hair was pinned up wit' spirals fallin' around her face an' neck. I couldn't take my eyes off her. Solana knew the effect she had on mufuckas, and I was sure she was gettin' a kick outta makin' a nigga speechless. My eyes were drawn to her cherry-red lips an' . . . My thoughts were interrupted by her heavily accented English.

"Poppi, chu have a present for me, yes?" She tilted her head to the side an' raised a perfectly arched eyebrow, peering at me through huge blue eyes and long, dark lashes.

I held the cake box up and nodded, still tryin' to find my voice. "*Sí*, you know I got you. Even added a li'l extra since y'all my best clients."

She smiled and gave me a huge warm hug, and then stepped to the side and waved her arm in a gesture for me to come in. The air was thick from way too much weed smoke and a swarm of Nag Champa incense she'd lit all over the place. Solana closed the front door behind me. There was no light source in the room; all of the windows were covered in thick expensive drapes, and I could make out candles as my eyes adjusted. Taking the box out of my hands, Solana glided over and perched on a white leather couch in front of a coffee table.

"Please, sit with me. Would chu like aqua or something?" She was settin' the coke out on the table and spreadin' out lines.

"Solana, ma. I can't stay. I've got business to take care of."

She leaned forward an' quickly made the first white line disappear up her pretty, bronzed nostril. Flinging her head back, she motioned for me to come do a line.

This was our custom; if it were anyone else I would have said hell no. The cool leather was feather soft as it sank beneath me. I took the rolled-up hundred dollar bill from between her long, manicured fingers. Leaning forward I did my line jus' as quickly as she had, closing my eyes and leaning my head back. I let myself relax, enjoyin' the familiar tingle that started at the top of my head and worked its way down my body. The thing with coke is that it's well known for makin' women horny as hell. I was pro'ly one of the few niggas in the world it had that affect on as well. My lips had started tinglin', more so than any other part of my body. I opened my eyes and my dick reacted before my brain even caught up. Solana was kissin' me, timidly, soft enough for my high ass to think it was jus' the coke affectin' me.

My senses felt heightened. I could smell everything from the incense to the fresh scent of Solana's shampoo, down to the slightest hint of her arousal. The heat from her skin radiated toward me and I could feel myself gettin' hot in return. My heart thundered in my chest and I focused on kissin' her back, losin' all the sense of urgency to leave that I'd felt earlier. She pulled back from my lips and eyed me intently; she was so close I could see the traces of powder that lightly dusted her nose. She half whined, half pleaded with me.

"Please, poppi, stay a little while. I've missed my black mamba." She accentuated her request with a pretty pout.

Black mamba was her pet name for daddy dick. The first time she called me that shit I thought she was jus' usin' that name 'cause I'm black; hell, I almost got offended. Never knew it was a damn type of snake 'til she broke it down for me. There was no way I was gonna disappoint her tonight. I did another line and felt energized. This shit was good!

"Bring ya fine ass here an' call me that poppi shit some more." Yo, I was higher than a kite and 'bout to lay into one of the most beautiful women in the world. My life was fuckin' perfect sometimes. Grabbin' Solana by the hair, I pushed her roughly from the couch onto the floor and clumsily fell with her. Thankfully our landing was cushioned by the thick carpeting. I'd managed to wedge myself in between her long, lean legs. Her robe had slid off of her shoulders, exposing tight pink rosebud nipples. I quickly drew one into my mouth and flicked my tongue across it. Solana moaned somethin' in Spanish and tried to reach the button on my pants. I grabbed her hands, pinnin' them above her head.

"You let poppi run this, ma. Relax," I told her. I was leanin' in to kiss her when a noise behind me caught my attention. I glanced over my shoulder and saw Miho's figure in the doorway. He'd been watchin' us.

"Damn, did you two start the party without me?" A thick white cloud of blunt smoke accented his words and he silently walked over and took a seat on the couch above us.

"*Ay dios mio,* Miho! *Debes estar bromeando!* Chu have to be kidding me!" Eyes ablaze, Solana was glaring up over my shoulder at Miho. She always said things twice when she was angry, once in Spanish and again in English. I guess it was for emphasis, but to my nigga ears it was the sexiest soundin' shit in the world. I ground my hips to regain her attention.

"Poppi, chu don't understand. He promised me at least half an hour." Solana was spoiled rotten and used to havin' her way. She was poutin' up at me, and I couldn't help myself. I kissed her hard, ignorin' Miho altogether.

Takin' a few hits from his blunt, he replied in that weed voice niggas use when they try to talk durin' an inhale.

"Mami, if chu want to play, we play by my rules, an' I can change them whenefer I choose." He coughed and muttered, "An' I choose to watch. Chu already know this." Miho sat back and crossed his arms over his chest as if he was provin' his point. His hand sliced through the air, motionin' for us to continue.

I was too high and too horny to care. I kept Solana's wrists hostage in one hand and undid my pants with the other. It was time to put in a li'l work. Solana's moans were the only thing I focused on as I handled my business right in front of her husband. She and Miho were bona fide real-deal swingers. Why the hell you think they my favorite clients? Miho was cursed wit' da baby dick so ere now and again he liked to watch me blow Solana's back out. Hell, I had a li'l exhibitionist in me. I didn't mind him watchin', long as he didn't come at me sideways. He was so infatuated with her that he actually gave her the okay to fuck otha niggas. I couldn't knock him for it. Solana was one bad mufucka.

# No News is Good News

## 9

The sound of a street sweeper woke me up out
of a light sleep. I couldn't have slept more than
two hours the whole night. Michelle wasn't even
a problem. I had to smile at myself for that bottle
of Nuvo I had sent over to our table at dinner last
night. My good girl only drank on special occa-
sions, and even then it's only that light-weight
girly shit like fuzzy navels or wine spritzers. The
last time I got her twisted, I ended up with a son.
She woke up when I came in just long enough to
ask where I'd been and seemed content when I
reminded her that I needed to deliver a package.

Just thinkin' about the ride home from the
restaurant had my shit gettin' hard all over
again. I was on the highway, eyes half closed,
fightin' the itis extra hard. Michelle had kicked
off her heels and had started runnin' her nails up
and down the side of my neck. She always knew

how to get me started. Next thing I knew she was leanin' over the center console and tellin' me, "Thank you for a lovely dinner." With every lick I could hear the wetness and feel the heat from her lips wrapped around my dick. Every now and again she would hum just a li'l, and I swore the vibration would run from my toes up to my damn eyebrows. Yeah, you got a few drinks in her and she started cravin' daddy dick. She the only bitch I'd ever known who get off from givin' head. That's one of the reasons she'd always been number one.

Michelle had already left, and she always took li'l man to daycare on her way to work. The house was quiet, givin' me time to go over my plan. You know what they say: "If you fail to plan, you are plannin' to fail."

That's the only reason I'd made it this long without gettin' picked up. After I got home last night I slipped Michelle's driver's license out of her purse. She didn't buy liquor and she damn sure betta not get pulled over for drivin' crazy with my son in the car. Outside of those reasons I couldn't see her checkin' for it all day.

I made my way into the other room to get her Social Security card out of the strong box. I was on my way into the kitchen when my phone buzzed again. I pulled it out of my pocket and slid my finger across the screen to enter my unlock code and check my texts. I'd only made the mistake once of trustin' a bitch around my phone. When a nigga was a young dude still new to the game, I was laid up with one of my old fuck buddies. She ain't know she was just pussy. Yo, I had this girl buyin' me shit, holdin' my stash; if you asked her she'd say she *was* wifey. Long story short, I woke up with this ho sittin' on my chest like on some shit straight outta a movie. She'd looked in my phone while I was asleep and saw I had four other bitches just like her and went the fuck off.

I didn't know where she found the screwdriver she used to stab me in my shoulder, but I ain't a snitch nigga. One hit and she was out cold. I let my boys deal with her. She even had the nerve to tell Derrick she was actually aiming for my heart, it was only coincidence that she missed when I tried to throw her off. I looked at that scar every morning to remind me of a woman's fury. No bitch got my full trust—not even Michelle.

I called Derrick's phone and he picked up on the first ring.

"Damn, nigga, lemme find out you sittin' on the phone now."

"Shit, nigga, that's only because I thought it was ya momma callin'." He laughed loudly in my ear.

"My nigga," I said in my most serious voice. "I done masterminded some shit that's gonna make you piss ya'self. Go grab Honey an' stop at Macy's. Pick up somethin' to make her look like a damn librarian or school teacher."

"Nigga, Honey right here. She had asked me to run her by the DMV so she could get her license. We'll meet up wi'chu in a bit." I was surprised that Honey had asked Derrick to help her with somethin' like that instead of callin' me, but then I remembered that I did ask him to drop her off at work last night, so it was only logical that she asked him to help her out today. I dismissed my paranoia; the pussy wasn't that good and the head wasn't nowhere near hot enough to make me trip like I was trippin'.

"All right, D. I'll see y'all's asses in a few."

Makin' my way back into the bedroom, I looked in my pants pocket for the money from the delivery to Solana. It wasn't there. A momentary panic coursed through me until I noticed the envelope sittin' on top of my dresser. I must have taken it out and forgot; I was pretty fucked up. I chuckled to myself and grabbed up the envelope. I'd decided to just tuck it in the closet for now, and noticed a purple dildo on the floor in front of the clothes hamper. It was nothin' I'd ever seen Michelle use before. As far as I knew she was too prim and proper to get herself off. She must have been on some new-age female empowerment shit or somethin'. Shakin' my head, I made a mental note to tell Michelle her housekeepin' abilities were getting kind of lax, and proceeded to get dressed and head out.

I picked out my favorite pair of khakis and an orange and white polo shirt, splashed my neck with a little Issey Miyake and grabbed my Edox watch. I prided myself on lookin' like a business nigga no matter what. I'm black and my name is Rasheed. That in itself is niggerish enough to make the cops think I'm suspect; no need to *look* suspect as well.

The one thing I'd always loved about being a city nigga—the opportunities. Summer smelled like money, winter felt like paper, and the spring and fall screamed chedda. I was about a block away from the club when my admirers and customers started tryin' to get at me. This bold, thick-ass li'l red ho walked up to the car as I pulled into my parkin' spot tryin' to do me favors. I told her stop by later for a real interview. Shit, I didn't maintain 'em but I'd train 'em and brain 'em quick. I needed to do a li'l ho'scaping anyway, switch out some girls so my clients didn't get bored.

I needed to check the drop from last night's business, and clear the girls' safes. As I walked in I was greeted by the familiar smell of stale alcohol and baby powder, but nothin' could cover up the smell of old sex and stripper sweat. I couldn't help but wonder what Danita was tellin' the cops, or not tellin' the cops for that matter.

It had been a good six years since I'd even heard her name. I had to admit, I was younger and even dumber, but not damn dumb enough. Me and Dee would get a suite and lock ourselves in for days at a time. We couldn't get enough of each other. I'd get a couple ounces of Kush and stock the fridge with bottles of Cristal; that was before niggas stopped fuckin' with it, and we would get smashed and fuck until a nigga was too sore to keep goin'.

Danita was the first stripper I ever dated, so a nigga was extra sloppy with it. I'm talkin' about goin' raw and not givin' a fuck if she was or wasn't on birth control. This was long before Trey, an' with my business just startin' to pop off—shit, a nigga felt *extra* lucky. I figured if she ever did get knocked up we'd just make a quick trip to the clinic and be done with it. I was so into Dee at the time it wouldn't have surprised me if she ended up bein' the Michelle in my life. But Danita was on some bullshit, and I was just glad

I caught wind of it before it was too late. I made a mental note to ask Honey if her birth control prescription needed a refill. I couldn't remember the last time she'd asked me for some change to get any, but I knew she was resourceful and could've just been usin' her own cash to get it.

I put all the money from the night before into the big safe in my office and logged into my computer to put a time stamp on the surveillance cam data. This way I wouldn't forget that I hadn't watched the footage from last night.

"My nigga," I said to myself, "time to head the fuck out. . . ." I was focused on how this shit was gonna play itself out. A nigga like me imagined every scenario and worked out a plan so there wouldn't be no damn surprises. Ain't no such thing as gettin' up early to catch me; a nigga just better not sleep at all. Just as my mind started to wander from plans and on to Ms. Red with the phat ass, Derrick rolled up with Honey in the passenger seat. This nigga couldn't have had better timing.

I felt myself gettin' jealous as Honey stepped out of Derrick's banana-yellow Dodge Charger, lookin' like Halle Berry, Gabrielle Union, and Jessica Rabbit all rolled into her li'l fine ass. They'd picked out a navy blue blazer with a matchin' blue skirt. Underneath the blazer was this silky cream top that had just enough buttons undone to expose the tops of her pretty, round titties, and made her caramel skin look like it was glowin' against the fabric. I was sure that was all Derrick's doing. To set the outfit off she had on a bright red belt with matchin' red pumps. There was no doubt in my mind those were Honey's contributions to the ensemble.

"Ohhh, baby." Honey started chatterin' before I could get a word in. "Thank you so, so much. This is Versace. I've never had *anything* this nice before." Honey was beaming and so excited over the new clothes. You sure as hell can't turn a ho into a housewife or a businesswoman, but you can dress her ass up like one.

"Girl, you lookin' right, right now." I couldn't tell her too much, ain't wanna blow her head up a whole damn lot. Ain't nothin' worse than a ho who knows her worth. You keep 'em feelin' worthless and they'll pay you to show you what they feel like they value is. Yeah, it's fucked up, but that's life.

"My dog, good to see you." I dapped up Derrick and gave him a quick rundown of what we was about to do. Honey had been listening to the convo intently. I could tell she was startin' to get nervous from the sweat beads on her upper lip.

"Daddy, what if they look at the ID, or ask me somethin' I can't answer?"

It's a fact of life, a ho is only as weak as the nigga who runs her. If I told Honey a flea can pull a tree, then she should be lookin' for a leash.

I looked this girl in her eyes and told her she's gonna be fine, when I sure as hell had no idea if this would work.

# Business Time

## 10

I decided we would all ride in one of my Benzes since it was less obvious than Derrick's yellow submarine, and we'd go two hours outside of town to a First Union Bank. This way I wouldn't have to worry about the teller recognizin' Michelle's name, or Honey for that matter. The bank would be closin' in half an hour and they would be in a hurry to just set up the account and carry they asses home. I handed Honey a thick envelope with six Gs inside. Her hands were shakin' a little and I realized I needed to calm her the fuck down so this would run as smooth as possible. I'd decided not to go in with her. In the event the shit went sour later on down the road I couldn't afford to be seen with her on a surveillance camera—I told you, a nigga stay thinkin'. I'd decided to just change the ATM PIN and request a new account number once we were set up.

"You lookin' like a real-deal accountant right now, girl. I might have to consider takin' you off the stage and givin' you a job in the club office." Derrick glanced at me with an eyebrow raised. I knew he would catch on; we thought too much alike.

"Y . . . you, playin' right? Baby, don't be messin' wit' me right now, it ain't funny."

I looked into the rearview and locked eyes wit' her. "Girl, you know I don't play when it comes to my paper or my pussy. Look at this like an initiation. You get this situated and you graduate from the stage. Hell, I'll even go 'head and get that car fa ya ass as a promotion gift." I could see Honey's eyes light up with the thought of finally havin' a car dancin' 'round in her head.

She squared up her shoulders, took a deep breath. "Well, nigga, let's hurry up and get this done then, so we can go car shoppin'."

"My neezy, you never fail to amaze me." Derrick was lookin' over at me in awe while we sat in the parkin' lot, waitin' on Honey to come out of the bank.

"Shit, Michelle is the one who gave me the idea. Nigga, this same shit happened at her bank and it took them fuckin' three months to sort that shit out, and that was only *after* the mufuckas cashed an illegal check. All our paper gonna look legit and the account is gonna re-volve like any other, so they won't have no rea-son to expect foul play. Worst come to worst, I'm not even connected. Anything go down, Honey takes the blame. As long as I keep her comfy in the pen I know she ain't rattin' a nigga out. She actually love my ass—she'll for real ride or die."

I'd fed Honey some bullshit story 'bout bein' a single career woman workin' wit' an accountin' firm. Even gave her a li'l leather day planner with all the info prewritten out so she wouldn't have to memorize anything while fillin' out the paperwork. The banks didn't question shit un-der ten Gs, but I told her the six Gs were her life savings she'd withdrawn from her prior account *if* they questioned that shit. Jus' as Honey came walkin' out of the bank my phone buzzed. It was Michelle, which was strange 'cause she rarely called when she was at work, but I was anxious to make sure everything went okay, and ignored the call to focus on Honey.

Honey walked over to the car, climbed into the back seat, and didn't say a word. I didn't want to seem overly anxious so I just started drivin'. Der-rick, on the other hand, couldn't stand the sus-pense and turned completely around in his seat.

"Damn, woman, what the hell happened?" For a split second Honey looked like she was about to tell us our worst fear, and then she broke into a full grin.

"I would like to go to the dealership now, thank you." She handed Derrick the day planner with the account info, ATM card, and deposit slip. She told me the PIN was 1215, same as the street address for the club. That was my girl. I was so proud of her I really did consider givin' her that office job, but I figured a new coupe and some daddy dick would keep her happy enough. I would just let her transport some product every now and again, and the car would actually be more like a biz investment. Yeah, I was definitely one thinkin'-ass nigga!

We stopped and ate at a small diner on our way back in town. As we were waitin' to be seated, I noted the few niggas up in there givin' Honey the once-ova. They promptly averted they eyes when they saw me lookin' back. Honey noticed none of this; she was too busy textin' away on a Black-Berry she'd just pulled out of her purse.

"Hol' up, how you go from no phone to havin' a BlackBerry in a day, and why the fuck I ain't got the numba?" I tried not to sound irritated but it really was botherin' me.

"Oh, daddy, I was gonna give it to you. I was so excited 'bout the clothes, and then I was so nervous 'bout my"—she paused to throw up finger quotation marks—"'initiation', I just forgot to even bring it up. One of the girls I met at that, ummm"—she glanced at Derrick for a sec and then continued—"that . . . *party* I told you about was damn cool, and suggested we keep in touch."

· Honey's answer seemed innocent enough, and I was all right for the moment. Besides she really ain't have a lot of close friends so one or two to keep her occupied when I was takin' care of home with Michelle couldn't hurt. I was in a much better mood after she texted me her number and the last four was a nigga birthday: 0801. We had a quick and uneventful meal. I checked in on Michelle and wasn't even surprised when she ain't answer. Most likely anotha one of her damn mind games, since a nigga ain't answer her call earlier. I checked the voice mail she'd left and felt the blood drain from my face. She was handling business at a branch outside of town and would be late getting home. She needed me to pick up Trey from daycare.

I kept repeating to myself that out of all the banks in and out of Hampton Roads, there was no way we could have been at the same bank today. I would have heard something by now if that was the case.

# Quiet Storms

## 11

We got back in town and I dropped Derrick off at his car. I was gonna take Honey to the club to get ready to start her shift, then decided to just get a room and celebrate a little since she really did do a decent job with the bank situation. Honey had gotten into the front seat and was textin' away on that damn BlackBerry as she'd been doin' all evenin'.

"Damn, girl, that betta not be anotha nigga. . . ." I really didn't mind her textin' 'cause it gave me time to think, but I just wanted to make sure she was still down for me and only me.

"No, baby, I know whose pussy this is." She looked at me with so much trust and affection, like a nigga could lose everything tomorrow and she would still be there.

It had started to rain and I was actually enjoyin' the quiet drive, with nothin' but the sound of the windshield wipers and Honey tappin' at her BlackBerry keys every now and again. I was really startin' to wonder who the hell she was carryin' on such an intense conversation with, but I didn't know if it was the suit she was wearin' or the feelin' of accomplishment, but my dick was startin' to beg for some attention. I pulled off the highway and took an exit toward the south side of town. It was rainin' harder now and lightnin' was shootin' across the sky like fireworks as one of those summer thunderstorms moved in.

Honey wasn't payin' any attention to where we were goin'. She was so busy textin' she didn't even notice that I'd pulled into a closed park. She finally looked up over that damn phone, and even though I was horny I was actually startin' to feel what I guess you can call jealousy. I mean, she'd just gotten the thing; was she textin' 'bout the bank job? Hell, maybe it *was* anotha nigga. I decided to make her pay for the way I was feelin'. You never let a bitch know when you really feelin' some kinda way or she'll use that shit to her full advantage. But there were always ways to get your point across.

"What's wrong, baby, where are we?" She was lookin' at me quizzically and I didn't say a word, just looked at her blankly until I started to see fear slowly creep into her eyes. That's what I wanted. I spoke very calmly and tried to hide the bulge that was startin' to grow from the excitement of the moment and the control I had over her.

"You love me." I didn't ask so much as say it like a statement.

I saw her fear startin' to ebb away.

"You know I do, baby. Is everything okay?"

I knew this area of town was secluded; the chances of anyone comin' out here were pretty slim. Trees lined either side of the driveway that snaked up to the park entrance, and once you made it through the park's gate it was almost like sittin' in the middle of a forest. There were a few park benches and picnic tables underneath a wooden shelter and for the most part it was pretty much peaceful.

"Come wit' me." I put my cell in the arm rest, shut off the engine, and opened my door. I could tell Honey wanted to say somethin', ask for an umbrella, complain about gettin' her Versace suit wet, but I just acted like it wasn't rainin' and waited for her to get out of the car, and she did with no further hesitation. I walked over, took her hand, and led her toward the picnic shelter with the picnic table under it. I picked Honey up and sat her on the edge of the table and stood between her legs. She could feel the heat from my dick strainin' against my khakis right up against her flesh; leave it to a stripper to be in two-thousand-dollar threads and not have on any damn panties. I smiled to myself. As I leaned in to kiss her she already knew what was 'bout to go down. I grabbed the back of her hair and leaned her head back so I could have full access to her neck.

She smelled like warm vanilla sugar and tasted just as sweet. I licked and sucked the rain from every inch of skin I had access to, from her collarbone upward to her earlobe, and was undoin' my pants and pullin' myself outta the slit in my boxers and khakis with my other hand. I stroked my dick for a second and let her hair go just long enough to roughly slide her ass closer to the edge of the table. I positioned myself and leaned forward, rubbin' the head up and down the folds of her outer lips, teasin' her pussy, slowly draggin' her moisture upward and rubbin' small circles 'round her clit.

She was moaning in my ear now, nibbling my earlobe in between sayin' my name. This was the only time she ever called me Rasheed. Any other time I was "baby" or "daddy" but when she really wanted it or when it was gettin' extra good, she called me by my name. I was still feelin' like I needed to remind her who she belonged to. Honey was about to get taught a new lesson.

I could feel her clit swelling as I maintained a steady rhythm rubbin' myself across it. Every time I'd slip lower like I was about to slide in, she'd hold her breath and close her eyes, but then I'd move back up and massage her clit some more with the head. I'd decided it's time she learn about the pleasure of pain. I almost laughed as a brief memory flashed my mind back to a time when I tried to go there with Michelle. She wasn't goin' for it and I never tried again. It always bothered me just a li'l that she could be so close-minded. But then I said to myself, *well that's part of the reason I'm fuckin' with Honey now.*

Lightnin' split the sky open and for a split second I wondered how safe it was to be under a tall wooden structure with my dick hangin' out. I figured to hell with it, a nigga gotta die someday, what be a betta way than gettin' some ass?

"Are you ready, baby?" I already knew the answer but I just wanted to hear her say it. I could smell her wetness and feel it hot and slippery on my hand and dick. Michelle never got this fuckin' wet for me. I didn't think I could remember any chick gettin' as wet as Honey did. I didn't hear an answer, so I tightened my hand in her hair and put my mouth up against Honey's ear.

"You want daddy to give you dis dick or not? I ain't hear you." I spoke though clenched teeth like I was angry for emphasis. She half moaned, half whispered, "Yes," and tried to nod, but I had her head held back by her hair. In that second I took a deep breath and drove myself deep into her flesh. My rigid heat seared the folds of her soft warmth and I wrapped the hair at the nape of her neck tighter around my fist. I gently used my tongue to trace a circle right where her shoulder and neck met as I gently began stroking a slow fire in her. I bit down hard on her neck, not hard enough to break the skin but hard enough to bruise her, hard enough to make that shit hurt and would be sore to the touch later.

It takes a certain kind of person to appreciate pain with pleasure and I almost lost it when she reacted by screamin' my name and lockin' her legs tightly around my waist, pullin' me deeper inside. Her fingernails were diggin' into my shoulders through my shirt, but I still kept my grip on her hair and used my mouth to lightly suck on the same sensitive area I had just abused as I let her feel the length of me stretchin' and slidin' deeper.

She was so close. I could feel her pulsin' and throbbin', squeezin' me tighter. I wasn't the one in control anymore, her muscles were milkin' me, almost forcin' me to release. I could feel my sac tightenin' and I knew we had to switch up or I definitely wasn't gonna be finishin' this race last. I lifted her small frame up without missin' a stroke.

"Hold on to me."

"Damn, daddy, wait a . . . Oooh fuck . . ." Honey was gone; there weren't any more words after that, at least none I could understand. We'd always been on a couch or had a bed available, so the whole standin' up shit was new to her. That's probably what I missed with Michelle. Even though it was good, it's like there was nothin' new about it, nothin' I could teach her and tons of shit she wasn't interested in learnin'.

I palmed an ass cheek in each hand and slid Honey's thick ass up and then back down my pole, slowly at first, until she surprised me by wrappin' her arms around my neck and pullin' me tight against her, movin' in a way I ain't know she knew how to move. I shifted her weight so that I had one arm holdin' her around the waist, and I used the other to once again take its position at the back of her neck. I tugged her hair gently, bringin' her face up from my shoulder.

"Look at me, baby. Look daddy in the eye when you takin' this dick." I looked into Honey's glazed eyes for a brief moment before kissing her deep, and I felt even more powerful as I drove myself deeper. I ended up kissin' her moans 'cause the shit was feelin' so good to her she couldn't even kiss me back. I moved my hands back to guidin' her ass and closed my own eyes for a second.

My biceps were startin' to burn and I could feel my neck tightenin' up, but none of that mattered because the tension buildin' up let me know I was about to let go so deep inside, I wouldn't be surprised if she could taste it. I could feel her legs startin' to shake as they tightened even more around my waist, and as I drove upward I pulled Honey down hard, and was surprised as shit when her whole body shook and she bit down on my shoulder just as hard if not harder than I'd bitten her. I felt her walls clenchin' around me with the first ripple of her release, and I had no choice but join her and pray my ass ain't fall over.

# B-side

## 12

It never failed. Whenever I needed Rasheed the most was when he absolutely refused to answer. There was no way I would have made it in time to pick up Trey from daycare and they charged all kinds of fees if you picked up your kid late. I never called Rah when I was at work, so you would have thought he would realize it must be important and answer. I was so glad Ris was able to go get Trey for me. It had been nearly six hours since I'd called Rasheed and still no word back from him. Sometimes I couldn't help but feel like I was doing everything all by myself.

That night at the house party I came face to face with the realization of what Rasheed actually did for a living. It was different when we were younger, before we had Trey and any real responsibilities. But now it just seemed too reckless, too much risk was involved. I did my best to stay at the party and have a good time but Larissa understood why I needed to leave. I was either going to go and knock on that woman's door, or wait at Rah's car until he came back outside. Neither of which would have been safe or smart—if he really was working. People who deal and do drugs are always armed and extremely paranoid. It would have hurt us both if I made a client of his feel like Rah was a bad source to deal with. I felt a little better when I saw the asshole who sped away in the black Beemer return to the house, but I still wanted nothing more than to get out of the area.

After Rah had come home smelling like weed and cheap incense I eased out of bed and checked his pants pockets. Sure enough there was an envelope with what could have been at least $50,000 inside. Why did he come home with so much cash on him, what if he would have gotten robbed or pulled over? Our rule was that he keep large sums of money in the safe at the club or one of his other establishments. He was getting lazy and it was starting to show. All kinds of questions had started plaguing me concerning Rah's safety. I knew I could easily be in danger just from being associated with him. I was beginning to worry more and more whenever he was out in the streets.

I called several more times and still no answer. Trey was staying with Ris for the night so I decided to call and check on him, and secretly hoped talking to Ris would calm my nerves.

"Well, hello, sunshine. You heard from idiot yet?"

"No. How's Trey? Is he asleep, did he eat?"

"Girl, me an' my li'l boyfriend are jus' fine. He's curled up in my bed knocked out. I suggest you come over an' hang out with us. We can have one big slumber party."

I was touched by her attempt to help cheer me up, but nothing was taking away the anxiety and stress of Rah not answering any of my calls. "I'm good, momma, thank you again. I might go out for a drive or something to clear my head, so call my cell if you need me." I needed a distraction. I dialed Rah a few more times, sent him a couple of texts, and then gave up for the night. He was where he was, doing whatever he was doing with whoever he was with. Maybe it was time I started to act like he did. I turned off my cell and dropped it in my purse. Grabbing my car keys off the table I walked out of the house. I needed some fresh air.

It was wrong, but I needed to go see the one person I knew would help make me feel better.

# Into the Lion's Den

## 13

A nigga was real upset. I was physically drained, wet, and thirty minutes from any close hotels. After we got back in the car Honey's ass was out cold. No more textin' whoever. I made sure she had no room or energy to even think 'bout that bullshit. As I drove to a hotel I actually debated on lookin' at her damn phone but figured it wasn't even worth it. She ain't give me a solid reason yet to doubt her, and if I looked it would make me feel like I was actually sweatin' her a li'l and wasn't even about to be on no shit like that.

I pulled my own phone out of the armrest. *Eighteen* mufuckin' missed calls and all from Michelle. She even texted me "9-1-1" but then went on to cuss me out and say she ain't need me in the next four texts followin', only to end by askin' if I would bring some cereal 'cause Trey ain't have anything in the house for breakfast. I shook my head tryin' to figure out what had her so fuckin' riled up and looked at the clock. It was still early. I could have Honey checked in and situated by ten-fifteen and still have time to head by the club to make sure erebody was actin' right before goin' home to see what the hell had Michelle trippin'.

I pulled up outside the club and was happy the parkin' lot was packed. I always had a spot reserved at the front, but Derrick's ugly-ass Big Bird mobile was in it. He must have figured I was gonna be tied up all night. It was cool, he was my boy; if it had been anybody else I'd have had they shit towed to the junkyard or set up at the police station and sold at auction before they knew what the fuck happened. I always kept a change of clothes in my office so I went in through the back. I was lookin' rough from my li'l excursion with Honey and really ain't want none of the brothas to see me like this. I had a back door built onto my office. In my line of business you never wanna be trapped with no way out. Not too many niggas eva been in my office to know there even was a door. I had a fake wall that looked like the room ended, but if you walked up to it you would see a thirty-inch gap that served as a small hallway to my door. I didn't use it often, but when I did best believe I made sure no one was around to see.

I couldn't believe the closest spot I could find was so far in the damn back that it took me nearly five minutes to walk to the club. I was tempted to call Derrick and tell him to move his shit, but figured since he'd been lookin' out I'd leave him be for once. I could hear Ludacris's "How Low" basing outside the door as I slid my key into the lock. I loved when Diamond danced to that. Shiiiit, that bitch would make her ass jump with the music and I swear ere nigga, even yours truly, would just stare at her, mesmerized. I was glad Honey wasn't workin' tonight. I started to feel a renewed tightening in my pants and hoped Ms. Red showed up. She might actually get a full-blown "interview." I was feelin' lazy and tired of doin' all the work. I wanted to be catered to for a change.

The door quietly opened to my office and I slid into the narrow walkway. God help a nigga, but if I ever got any bigger I would neva be able to use this shit. I started toward my office, but stopped when I heard talkin' and smelled one of my cognac-preserved cigars bein' fired up. I held my breath and listened.

"Nah, baby, I'm not upset. I told you I understand, remember? Give me about thirty minutes and I'll meet you, okay?" After hearing Derrick's hushed voice I moved in as usual. He was the only mufucka other than me and the contractors who knew that door was there, and he still jumped like he'd seen a ghost when I stepped in.

"Wow, nigga, you scared somebody gonna sneak up on you and take that ass or what?" I was all ready for his comeback but Derrick really seemed flustered and jumped off the phone. If I was crazy I would actually say he was more surprised to see me than he shoulda been, but I pushed that thought to the side.

"What the fuck, you silent ninja now? Creepin' up on mufuckas when they tryin'a relax or som'n, nigga?" Derrick dapped me up and stepped back. A grin spread across his face and I already knew he saw the wet stain on the front of my khakis from Honey's downpour earlier.

"Don't say nu'n to me, and I won't ask what broad you was in here on the phone boo-lovin' wit', nigga. Shit, you pro'ly jumped 'cause you was tryin'a pull ya dick back in ya pants. I betta not find any damn stains up under my fuckin' desk or it's war, nigga."

Derrick laughed and made his way to the office door. I went into my bathroom, opened my closet, and pulled out some fresh black slacks and a grey and white Dior button-down. I had the bathroom and closet put in 'round the same time I was messin' with Dee.

Damn. There that girl was, runnin' 'cross my mind again. There were some nights when I would pull her off the roster for the evening and lock her in here with me. I swear we fucked on ere piece of furniture and ere inch of carpet in this bitch! It was to the point where we would have to wait until the A.M. to leave or bear the shame of niggas and hoes watchin' us walk out, clothes and hair tore the fuck up from the shit we did to each other. That's when I'd decided a shower would be a pretty good idea. Even when meetin's ran long or I had a late night, I could always freshen up.

It didn't take me long to shower, and I winced when I wiped the mirror to shave and saw my reflection. Times like this made me wish I was a dark mufucka. God blessed me with this silky golden or "light bright" complexion, as Derrick liked to jokingly call it. The last thing I needed when I went home to Michelle was the bright red and purple bite marks on my shoulder. I turned and saw several red lines scratched across my back from Honey's nails. My baby had a li'l fight in her. I was silently enjoying the thought of other things I might have to try with her while I came up with a reasonable explanation for Michelle.

I checked my phone: no missed calls and only one text from Honey that said, "Is daddy comin' back?" Damn, this girl was insatiable. I'd left her in the hotel damn near sleep before the key hit the door and she woke up ready for round two. My thoughts were interrupted by a knock at the office door.

"Enter." I figured Derrick had sent Annette or one of the other girls to come check on me, so imagine my surprise when I turned and saw li'l Ms. Red with the phat ass from earlier.

"Hey, big sexy, you asked and here I am."

She spoke slowly with a sensual and kinda deep voice that reminded me of Toni Braxton. It automatically made me wonder if I could make it go higher. I didn't respond. I raised an eyebrow and watched her walk toward me. She wasn't shy, she wasn't awkward. Damn, I had to admit this was a drastic difference from Michelle's familiarity and Honey's innocence.

"I guess you already know who I am, and what I do?" I asked every girl this question. A bitch couldn't fuck with me if she couldn't understand or accept that I was surrounded by ass and titties nearly all day every day. She narrowed her grey-green eyes and shook her head yes, seductively pullin' the straps to her dress down her shoulders. I pretended not to pay her any mind, but was in all actuality studyin' her every move. There was somethin' 'bout her that seemed familiar. I tried but couldn't place her face with anyone I'd fucked with or interviewed lately.

This wasn't new to me. When you have what I had, you get used to women who are willin' to do whateva the fuck it takes to get your affection, attention, or in other words, your paper. I knew this bitch was no different than all the others and I wasn't finished testin' her yet. I was surrounded by pussy, I sold pussy, I owned pussy, so when it came to stickin' my dick in it—believe it or not, I did get selective. I walked over to my desk and sat behind it. I always kept a bottle of Remy or Henny for rough nights. I poured myself a glass and watched Ms. Red finish undressing.

I can't lie. She was bad. I looked at a lot of bodies and it's rare that I saw any without any work done or that were minus the tell-tale signs from havin' kids. Her body was fuckin' perfect. Her breasts were full and slightly pointed upward, and I loved bitches with full hips and thighs, and she had it all. I felt myself gettin' excited as I pictured her spread out on my desk, but I squelched that shit; she ain't passed all the test yet. Daddy dick ain't for erebody.

"Come over here. I need to ask you somethin'." I took a sip from my glass and felt the cognac heat up my throat and chest, and warm my stomach. Ms. Red walked around the side of the desk slowly, eyes focused on mine. Like a huntress. There was no shyness, no nothin'.

"So what type of shit are you into?" I asked. I was eye level with firm, erect nipples and did my damnedest to avoid lowering my gaze toward the soft curve of her waist and bare, perfectly waxed pussy. She didn't even blink and answered me in that same sultry tone.

"I don't know what you mean. I'm into you right now and I think you should get undressed so you can get *into* me."

If I were a weaker nigga with a green-eyed model-lookin' beauty standing in front of me naked, this conversation would have never been happenin', but somethin' jus' ain't seem right with shorty. I couldn't put my finger on it. I took another sip from my glass.

"You don't look like you'd have a problem gettin' any nigga on the street, what makes me such an exception that you in here ready to throw down an ain't even asked my name?" Exactly what I thought. The bitch ain't even have the nerve to answer me. When a nigga knows, a nigga knows. I knew exactly why she was here. I explained to her, "I been doin' this shit for a while and it's almost like when someone walks into a store and the salesman knows exactly what they're lookin for." I reached into my desk and pulled out what I liked to call "pick your poison." I had everything from cigarettes on up to heroin and coke stashed in a small mahogany box in my desk.

Growin' up my mother worked out of state so my auntie raised me. I grew up watchin' this woman shoot herself up with my lunch money, book money, hell sometimes the bitch would sell my clothes and shoes if someone was buyin'. On more than one occasion she offered me sex. Anything that would get me to give in and give her the money to go get fucked up. I never told my mom. I didn't want to make her feel any worse for leavin' me with her fucked-up sister than she'd already felt. I was so young and stupid. I had no problem lettin' my aunt suck me off for a couple of crack rocks; hell, head is head. A man can only say no so many times before it turns into a yes. My boys even smashed once or twice in exchange for ten or twenty dollars. I watched my aunt degrade herself to ho'n for her habit. To this day, I can't seriously fuck with a woman who smokes a cigarette or does anything harder than weed. Don't get it twisted, though, I can fuck all day, but if she got a habit she can't be anything more than a casual fuck. Rule number three of supply and demand.

I undid the twenty-four-karat gold clasps on the mahogany case in which I kept every drug addict's dream. There was an almost immediate change in her demeanor. The calmness was gone, and a sheen of sweat formed on her forehead and upper lip. Damn, this nigga was *good*. This ho wasn't nothin' but a damn fiend. Before I could even get the box completely open, she reached across me and grabbed a Baggie that held a few crack rocks and a pipe. I didn't bother stoppin' her. Why waste the energy fightin' her for a li'l crack? She wasn't going to do much with that pipe hypnotizin' her. I'd just let the boys come in and drag her ass out. No point gettin' my hands dirty behind some crack ho.

I reached under my desk and hit my "nigga, get in here" button. Yep, just like the ones they use at banks to signal a robbery. Michelle had given me that idea. If niggas ever tried to rob me or get stupid, that was Derrick and Big Baby's cue to get their asses in here. It was rigged to a red light outside my office door. Ms. Red sat cross-legged in the floor right in front of my desk, lightin' up like she was the only one in the room.

I sat back and waited for my boys to come get her. After a few minutes, I hit the button again. Normally, they would have responded within a few seconds. I kept a forty-five in my left-hand desk drawer as well as in the end table closest to the bathroom. I looked at ol' girl, but could tell she really wasn't gonna be any more of a threat. She was sittin' on the floor butt-ass naked, eyes rollin' back in her head.

I pulled my phone out of my pocket and dialed Derrick's number, no answer. I was makin' my way to the door when I tripped over her clothes. My foot hit somethin' harder than a dress or a shoe and I bent down and was in complete shock as I picked up a pearl-handled handgun. It was loaded and everything. I stuffed it in my pocket and rushed out into the club.

I saw Derrick before he saw me and noticed the nigga was steady glancin' at his cell, yet he ain't answer when I'd just hit his ass. Big Baby was nowhere to be seen so I started to make my way over to Derrick.

I made my way through the maze of bodies. Dancers were tryin' to make small talk, niggas tryin' to dap me up. No one was gettin' outta my way fast enough. I bumped into Annette, declined a drink or whatever the fuck she was tryin' to offer me, and looked back up to see Derrick approachin' me.

"Nigga! You ain't see me hittin' you? My office. Now!"

I didn't wait to see if he was followin' me or not. I marched my ass back to where I'd left ol' girl. We walked in and I was stupefied; the bitch was gone along with my damn goodie box.

# More Than Coincidence

## 14

No one, and I repeat, not one muthafuckin' person had seen this chick come or go. I was startin' to feel like my day was goin' so good that I'd inadvertently pissed Murphy off and now all his laws were smackin' me in the face.

Before I left the club to go home, Derrick let me know that he might need to cut out early and that two of the brothas were catchin' hell on the street. Apparently, there were one or three overdose incidents and all of 'em were loyal customers. In the drug community, a heroin overdose can either work in your favor or it can work against you. Now addicts were either gonna flock to the shit thinkin' we got the purest product on the market and it's so potent it's dangerous. Or, they were gonna be scared we cuttin' our shit down too much and they'd buy from someone else. I told him we would look into the shit in the mornin'. All I wanted right now was to go home and have Michelle rub a nigga back. I chuckled to myself. *On second thought, let's stick wit' the temples.* My back was in no condition for her to see. I had Derrick drop me off at my car since I was parked damn near half a mile away.

"Yo, nigga," Derrick called out as I got out the car. "Want me to go check ya back seat for any mighty midget assassin bitches?" He was laughin' at his own joke and slappin' his knee.

My life was possibly threatened and this nigga had to be the one with the jokes. I shook my head and frowned, not really feelin' comedic at the moment. "Nah, my dude, somethin's up an' the fact that she got a fuckin' gun through security should be botherin' you, too." I walked over to my car, sneakin' a glace around me while unlockin' the driver side door. I was tryin' to convince myself ol' girl was just a druggie and I jus' happened to be a dealer, and that was the only connection—but sometimes the hardest person to convince is ya'self.

I drove home in silence, not really lookin' at the road or signs. I was on autopilot. Big Baby called but I ain't answer. My phone beeped when he left me a voice mail. I was surprised my shit wasn't full. I pulled up into my driveway, anxious to see my son, even if he was asleep. Where the fuck was Michelle? For a second I thought I'd pulled up to the wrong damn house. This couldn't be right. I looked at the clock. It was damn near 3:00 A.M. Where was she and where the hell was my son? I walked through the dark, cold house realizin' that their ass really wasn't home. I remembered her callin' me earlier when I was with Honey, textin' me 'bout some fuckin' cereal, and now this? *Oh.* I stopped in my tracks an' smirked in the dark. This bitch was playin' hardball. I guessed eighteen ignored calls drew the line for her. When I'd noticed no one was home I'd instinctively pulled my cell out of my pocket, ready to speed dial Michelle's number. I sighed into the darkness and turned off my cell, laying it to rest on the kitchen counter. I'd had enough for one night. I was starting to feel worn out. I didn't even bother undressing or showering; I went into the bedroom and lay across the bed fully clothed.

"Rasheed, get up." I heard a woman's voice pullin' me from a dreamless sleep. I turned from my back onto my side, away from the disturbance.

"Damn, Honey, give daddy like twenty more minutes, okay?" Before the words were completely outta my mouth, realization set in and I remembered where I was. *Fuck!*

"Nigga, I ain't ya damn honey. It's almost noon and you've got company."

Michelle didn't catch it. *Whew.* For once I was that glad she was in a pissy mood. I sat up and rubbed the sleep outta my eyes. "Who's here?" There weren't too many mufuckas who knew where I lived. For someone to show up meant it was serious. Michelle had her back to me, puttin' away laundry. She was doin' her damnedest not to answer me. I wanted to ask where the hell she went las' night, but figured whatever it was that brought someone to my crib was more important.

"My dude, you know I wouldn't come ova here if it wasn't important." Derrick was standin' in my livin' room in the same clothes he had on last night, unshaved and lookin' like he either had one helluva good night, or just a plain ol' helluva night.

"Me an' Big Baby been blowin' you up since las' night. There's somethin' we gotta handle at the club." I could hear Michelle comin' toward the front room and decided to carry our convo outside. I was silent while I slid on my shoes and tried to remember where the hell I'd set my phone. It was on the counter where I'd left it, dead since I hadn't put it on the charger.

Derrick followed me onto the front porch. Damn, it was already hot out.

"All right, nigga, what's the emergency?" I was prepared for the worst, mentally settin' myself up to leave town, set up a hit, possibly even do time. When you're involved in a lot of shit you always gotta be ready for the flies. They always come, and they come at you from all directions.

"Word is they cuttin' Danita a *serious* deal if she'll give you up. She said she won't talk if you'll work somethin' out wit' her. T, from the precinct, dropped me a line, sayin' they got a new chief an' he gunnin' fa any nigga in there acceptin' pay fa favors. If a cop so much as piss crooked, this nigga in there cuttin' throats."

All fell silent while I processed this new twist of fate. This was unexpected but it wasn't the worst. I knew I'd think of somethin'.

"All right." I put my hand on Derrick's shoulder. "You my boy, you the fuckin' co-captain of this ship. Ain't no ship with two of the trillest mufuckas in the world gonna go down 'causa one gotdamn white boy or an outta work ho. This ain't the *Titanic*. B, calm the fuck down." I looked my boy in the eye, the same nigga who ditched high school with me eight years ago 'cause we had the same vision. Instead of cuttin' class to get fucked up or chase pussy, we decided to make niggas pay us so they could come to the crib and do whateva. By this time my mom had moved back, but I still stayed with my aunt. My momma, not used to raisin' a son, came back when I was fourteen and wanted to raise a nigga like I was still in diapers. At least she made an honest attempt at us havin' a family. My aunt, on the otha hand, was easy. Get her doped up and the crib was my castle. We were both only sixteen when we started out. Look at us now. I ain't planned on lettin' that change for no one.

"Look, let me change up an' I'll meet you at the club in like thirty, a'ight?"

I didn't wait for Derrick to reply, and headed back inside outta that damn heat. A nigga's balls was startin'a sweat. I could hear the shower runnin' in the bathroom. I walked into Trey's room. My li'l man was out cold, takin' a nap in his "big boy" bed. I smiled and kissed him on the forehead, silently promisin' him I had our lives under control. As I left and closed the door I could smell nectarine or melon, some kinda sweet-scented fruity shit driftin' down the hallway. It was time to get to the bottom of Michelle's disappearin' act. I opened the bathroom door and enjoyed the warm rush of steam as it hit my face. As much as a nigga hate to be hot I sure as hell enjoy hot showers.

"Who takes a shower at almost one in the afternoon?" I closed the bathroom door and posted up against it, starin' at Michelle's frame through the shower glass. No response.

"Funny, you had a mouthful when we had a audience, an' now you ain' got shit to say, huh?" I watched while Michelle ignored me and lathered her arms and neck. Shit, I was actually enjoyin' the show, even though I was still a li'l peeved. Michelle turned her back to rinse and I took off my shoes and undid my pants.

"Nigga, what you doin'?" I slid my body behind Michelle's and wrapped my arms around her. She tried to slap my hands away.

"Rasheed, this ain't the time. Get out, I'm not even fuckin' playin' wi'chu right now."

I tightened my reverse bear hug and rested my chin on her shoulder. She was tensed up, ready to fight, but God she felt good. Out of all the bitches I'd eva fucked wit', she was one of the few who just *felt* right. Not only was she thicker than a mutucka, but she was tall. I was excited afta Trey was born when she worked out, toned herself back into shape. She still managed to keep what I liked to call "dem baby titties" and didn't lose any of her ass. I closed my eyes and exhaled.

"Baby, what are we doin?" I felt her body relax jus' a li'l as she lowered her head.

"It's not 'we' anymore, Rasheed, there's *you* and then there's me and your son."

I felt my chest tighten from the pain in her voice.

"Chelle, you know what I gotta do to keep us betta than comfortable. To make it so Trey don't have to do what his daddy do when he grow up." Michelle's hair was pinned up, exposing all of her neck. I took my chin off her shoulder and placed my lips at the back of her neck, pullin' her body closer into mine. I waited for an objection, a "but," or a "why?" Instead, she stood there and silently cried.

"Baby, one day I'ma turn the club an' erethang ova to D. I'ma retire an' we gonna get old an' sit on the porch . . ."

Michelle finished the last part with me. "An' rock in our rockin' chairs gettin' blitzed offa boxed wine."

We both giggled. The first time we got into that argument that ere nigga who don't wanna get married gotta have, those were my exact words to let her know I wasn't goin' anywhere.

"Rasheed, I only see you a few times a week—I miss you. Last night, you ignored every call and I felt like I ain't mean shit to you, like I ain't got nothin' on whoeva you're with, or whateva you're doing. I packed up Trey an' . . ."

I didn't need to hear any more. I knew I was wrong and, in the process of me bein' a selfish mufucka, I'd made my angel suffer—again. I didn't even care to know where she went or who she stayed with. I just wanted to make it right.

The bathroom was steamed up, lookin' like the inside of a cloud. I could feel the roundness of Michelle's ass pressin' into me, and the heat from the water was relaxin' to us both. I rubbed my lips across the back of her neck.

"I'm so sorry, baby." That was her spot. I felt every ounce of resistance leave her body as I continued to alternate runnin' my lips across the back of her neck and goin' back the same way my lips had come wit' my tongue.

Michelle lowered her head, turnin' her neck wit' my mouth. She let out a sigh and slid her hand behind her in between our bodies to grab my dick. I was already rock solid. She stroked upward, applyin' jus' the right amount of squeeze while rotatin' her hand and then goin' back down. I dragged my lips from the back of her neck and sucked on her earlobe while my hands went to cup her full, heavy breasts, slidin' her hard nipples between my fingers. I laughed to myself. *She betta be thankful I'm such a ambidextrous mufucka.* I released one of her nipples and ran my hand downward, lettin' my nails lightly graze her smooth, flat stomach 'til I reached my destination and parted her lips. My baby was ready. I let my finger glide across her clit and eased one inside. Chelle sucked in a sharp breath as her pussy adjusted and moistened aroun' my finger. Damn, even with the hot water all over us she still felt hotter. I brought my finger up to her mouth, provokin' her to taste herself. She didn't skip a beat and even swirled her tongue 'round it inside her mouth, lickin' it dry. I grabbed her chin, turned her head toward me, and teased her at first by nibblin' her bottom lip before finally kissin' her and lettin' myself enjoy how good her tongue tasted wit' her on it. Michelle was strokin' me somewhere I wasn't ready to be yet. I reached down and moved her hand, makin' her beg.

"Baby, please?"

That was all a nigga needed to hear. Usually when bitches wanted it like this, I'd have to bend my knees or squat to get it jus' right, but not wit' Chelle, we always jus' fit. I could feel my pulse throbbin' in my dick as I leaned her forward slightly and slowly guided my way into her heat. Once I was completely inside I stopped. Frustrated, Michelle sucked her teeth on the verge of a complaint.

"Unh unh, woman, don't even start. Lean back a li'l." As soon as her back was pressed flat against my chest an' the back of her head was restin' on my shoulder, I braced myself against the shower wall, covered her mouth wit' my hand, and drove myself upward, diggin' even deeper into her heat. I'd wrapped my arm 'round her waist to support her weight 'cause, jus' as I'd expected, her knees buckled and she let out a cry that was muffled by my hand.

The club was gonna have to wait. Everything was gonna have to hold off a li'l longer 'til I was done makin' Michelle forget how much she was hurtin'. I reached 'round her and turned off the water.

"Go lay on the bed, on your stomach." She didn't say a word and climbed out the shower. A nigga was 'bout to put in some work. I glanced at the clock on the dresser to see how far off schedule I was. We had plenty of time. I waited for Michelle to lie out completely and then I covered her wet body with mine. She tried to get up on her knees first before trying to roll over and face me, but I stopped her by bearin' my weight down and pressin' my chest into her shoulder blades. I wanted complete control. I traced the shape of her ear with my tongue, and let her feel my dick regainin' its stiffness pressed up against the small of her back.

"Tell me what you want, baby." I wanted her to say som'n dirty, ask me to do somethin' different. She turned toward me and looked me in the eye.

"Daddy, all I ever wanted was you."

For a minute I ain't know how the fuck to respond. It always fucked with me when Chelle called me "baby" or "daddy." A nigga done fucked up so much that she always seem guarded, like showin' me affection or sayin' somethin' nice would eventually come back and bite her in the ass.

"Baby, you got me. Stop worryin' so much." My niggas, this is what I like to call variety. I got one bitch gettin' me off when she say my name, and anotha gettin' me off when she don't. I held Michelle's gaze and, for a second, it felt like I could fix us. I could be faithful, treat her right. My voice caught in my throat.

"Damn. I'm so sorry, baby," and I really meant it. I kissed her shoulder, neck, forehead, and decided she was ready for this dick-down.

"Spread ya ass fa daddy." Chelle knew exactly what I meant. She reached back with a hand on the side of each cheek and parted all that ass outta my way. I supported my weight with one hand and guided my dick with the other. She started squirmin' her ass toward me, tryin'a force me inside, so I gave her what she wanted. I couldn't believe how long it'd been. I ain't remember her bein' this fuckin' tight or gotdamn hot. My breath hissed out between my teeth. Chelle put her face in the pillow and was tellin' me she loved me in between callin' Jesus. Pro'ly said she loved Jesus too. Ere time a nigga went deep she'd let go of that ass and I'd grab her hands and put 'em back, demandin' she "hold it fa me." The sun was comin' through the curtains of our bedroom window and I let myself enjoy the faces she was makin'. Our sheets were some deep purple-colored shit she picked out and her caramel skin looked fuckin' flawless up against 'em. Most women don't realize one important thing 'bout niggas: we visual as hell! Why the fuck you think porn stores, Web sites, hell even strip clubs make so much money? 'Cause niggas like to see! Chelle loves it wit' the lights off, so seein' her like this wit' her hair all lose, tanglin' roun' her face and neck, was bringin' out my inner porn star. I just prayed we ain't wake up Trey.

I got into a serious rhythm and gave up on her holdin' her ass, 'cause she wasn't holdin' nothin' but the sheets between her teeth. She was gettin' close. Her pussy was grippin' the hell outta me and with each thrust my balls were startin' to get that tight, full feelin'. I lay down flat against her back and circled my arm under her, grabbin' her throat. She might not have liked bitin', but she sure as hell ain't mind chokin'.

There's somethin' 'bout that shit, maybe it's the control or the fear of death if a nigga squeeze too tight, I'm not sure. But that was it, I felt her body tense beneath me and her muscles tightened hard aroun' my dick as she screamed words I couldn't make out into the pillows and started to shake. I gave one last thrust, fightin' hard against her grip that had me caught up like a hot velvet sleeve. I pulled out. The heat from my hand shielded me from the sudden temperature change as I closed my eyes and stroked myself, sendin' a full, hot flood of whiteout 'cross her ass and lower back—Michelle, unlike Honey, didn't like a nigga to cum inside her. She barely tolerated it when I came anywhere on her body. I had to hop up and grab a washcloth or towel and clean it off ASAP or she'd catch an attitude. You would think that after years of bein' together she'd try to get over that shit.

In the time it took me to grab a washcloth, Chelle was out cold. *Yep,* I thought, feelin' smug, *that's what that monsta dick do to 'em.* We used up all the hot water, so ironically I took a quick cold shower and threw on some clothes. I peeked in on Trey, who was surprisingly still asleep, grabbed a sandwich and my phone, and headed to the club.

# Daddy Daycare

## 15

I'd been on the road for 'bout twenty minutes before my phone was charged enough to turn on. I was calculatin' in my head how much money I'd pro'ly missed by not bein' available. When I could finally get into my inbox there were three "9-1-1" texts from Big Baby, one from Derrick askin' if I was at the crib yet or with Honey, and one from Honey that read, "ok, well gudnite." Guess she finally figured out I wasn't comin' back. I pulled up to the club and saw D's obvious-ass Mello Yello mobile but no one else. I suddenly remembered Danita's deal and wondered what the hell she wanted in return for her silence, and what made her think I would compromise when it would pro'ly be cheaper to jus' have her taken out.

I walked into the club and went about my usual routine. I'd cleared the first three safes before I noticed a pile of coats on the floor on the side of the stage. Somebody musta been in here gettin' some ass after hours las' night.

Derrick walked out of the kitchen with a plate of leftova wings from last night.

"You know, Big Shirley was pro'ly savin' those for her warm-up tonight." I was referrin' to Shiree, one of our top earners. This bitch had the phattest ass, the thickest Coke-bottle shape, and she ate like her ass had its own mufuckin' stomach! Playfully, I named that monster ass "Big Shirley." She would walk by and ya boy would be like, "Hi, Shiree, how ya doin', Big Shirley?" I done seen Shiree stab a hole in anotha bitch back wit' a stiletto ova some damn onion rings.

"They ain't fa me, an' she told me I could have 'em. We been waitin' for the last two hours, nigga. What happened to thirty minutes?"

I was 'bout to remind Derrick who the fuckin' "captain" of this ship was but I was still stuck on "we" part of his sentence. "What the fuck you mean, 'we' been waitin'?" I saw movement out of the corner of my eye by the stage and was 'bout to make my way to the office for my burner.

Derrick walked toward the stage. "Big Baby said he wandered in las' night right after we left."

It wasn't until then that I saw the li'l scrawny kid who had apparently been sleepin' on a pallet made from old, unclaimed coats. He cautiously approached us, crusty-eyed and still groggy. My first thought was that one of these stupid bitches left his ass in the car while they worked, but they woulda collected him by the end of the night. Someone had to be lookin' for him. He was wearin' Rocawear blue jeans and a Coogi polo shirt. They were a little big on him, but people who neglect their kids don't dress 'em from head to toe in name-brand labels.

"What the fuck, D? Why ain' somebody take him to a shelter or the police station? What, this look like *Daddy Day Care* to y'all niggas? That ain't a fuckin' puppy, it's a kid, now get him outta here!"

I started to walk toward my office. I wasn't expectin' to hear any objections. I was shocked when Derrick walked over and blocked my path. His tone was angry and he had the nerve to grit his teeth as he spoke. Like he ain' know a mufucka would snatch him up and straighten him the fuck out quicker than hummingbirds fuck.

"Nigga, his *momma* sent him here. Danita. Nigga, *she* locked up an' ain't got no one else to watch out for him. She promisin' she won't talk if you'll look out for her only son. Given y'all's history an' the shit she know 'bout our operation, at this point I think it's fair to say we can't shut her up. If she decide to talk, too many of the blues we pay off scared to do any favors an' we got no way of gettin' to her, so let's jus' make her happy and find the li'l nigga a spot."

Somethin' told me I shoulda killed that bitch. Now she was makin' demands? I ain't even know she had a son. I didn't like ultimatums and I damn sure didn't negotiate. But I was a calculatin' mufucka. If Dee's son was under my care, it was pretty obvious she wouldn't dare breathe a word 'bout anything to anyone.

"Li'l nigga." I walked toward the boy who was watchin' us intently. I was sure he'd heard our convo. He knew what was up. As I approached him, I felt some of my edge soften. He had to be 'bout eight, scrawny as hell, with curly black hair. Hell, I had a son too, and he reminded me of Trey.

"Li'l nigga, what's ya name an' how old are ya?" He looked up at me and my breath caught. He had her light brown, slanted eyes, thick, dark lashes, square chin—he was his momma's son. I almost felt ashamed of what I did to her face after seein' it reincarnated on him. But what's done was done.

"So you ain't gonna ans'a me?" He was still silent, starin' at me blankly. I was on the verge of gettin' pissed. . . .

"Five. Sir."

I could barely hear his shaky reply.

I was six four and he stood almost to my waist. I woulda sworn he was older. I felt myself calmin' down. It was bad enough he had a ho for a momma, some trick he pro'ly ain't even knew for a daddy, and now this.

"D, he stays wit' you until we figure somethin' out, so go ahead and send word to his momma."

# All Closed Eyes Ain't Sleep

## 16

I'll tell you what, a nigga's work ain't neva done. After Derrick left with the kid, I placed a few business calls. Looked like there wasn't gonna be a count today. Apparently sales were down due to those bad batch scares and anotha one of my niggas was picked up afta one of the damn fiends who got a bad hit decided to drop dime on who sold it to 'em. I put my cell down on the bar and looked aroun' the empty club. This was my empire. I'd made a lot of money. Maybe it was time I got out while I was still on top. Not quit, jus' retire. My phone lit up. It was Honey.

"Hey, daddy, I miss you. I gotta work tonight? Are you gonna pick me up, 'cause I need to grab some things from the house."

I forgot I'd left Honey at the damn hotel. Yeah, she really needed that car, 'cause a nigga was not feelin' a drive 'cross town and back. I cleared my throat.

"I got a betta idea. How 'bout you take tonight off an' we go shoppin', maybe grab some food or see what kinda Jacuzzi that hotel workin' wit'?" Jus' then Michelle beeped in. "So, go get ready, I'ma be there in a few." I switched over to Michelle. "Hello, sleepin' beauty. Glad to see I ain' put ya ass in a coma."

Chelle laughed and I could hear Trey in the background yellin' for me. Suddenly all I wanted to do was be home with my family.

"I'm cookin' lasagna tonight. Maybe you can skip workin' an' come spend some time with me an' Trey?" She sounded so hopeful.

I had a flashback to our shower and her lyin' on the bed in the sun. "Baby, Derrick had to go handle some biz so I'm runnin' the club tonight. Let me jus' get us open an' I'll be there soon as I can get a nigga in here to close it down for me, okay?" I could tell she was disappointed with my answer. I knew I couldn't fuck up right now; a nigga was on probation.

"Okay, Rasheed. I'll just see you when you get home."

I hung up and called Big Baby as I started walkin' out the door. He was gonna have to run this ship tonight. There was a car dealership that ran money for me when I needed clean bills. We also had product stashed in the door panels of a few cars for out-of-state runs and dry spells; that's when good shit gets scarce in the area. This was gonna work out perfect. I could give Honey one of those to drive and we would be even without me eva breakin' bread. I hit my boy Roman and let him know I was on the way.

I pulled up at the hotel and called to let Honey know I was outside. I didn't get an answer. While I parked the car I thought, *why it feel like I'm always fuckin' or fetchin' somebody?* I was outside Honey's room and was 'bout to knock, but heard her on the phone.

"I wish I could come help you too, but he on his way to get me now. We goin' shoppin'." She paused and giggled. "Well I guess you gon' have to put some ice on it then, huh?"

Who the fuck was she talkin' to? I ain't want anyone to walk up on me eavesdroppin' outside her door, so I knocked and listened as she lowered her voice. "He here. Text me okay?"

Honey opened the door, excited to see me.

"Hey, daddy!" She jumped toward me for a hug and circled her arms aroun' me.

I didn't hug her back. "I called to tell you I was outside, why ain't you answer?" I swore on my life, if this bitch was fuckin' anotha mufucka . . .

"Huh. Oh, I was on the phone wit' my girl." She walked over to the bed and started gatherin' up her purse.

I walked up behind her and grabbed her roughly by her shoulders. I knew I was fuckin' up. My jealousy was gettin' the best of me. I was showin' too much emotion.

"Don't fuckin' lie to me. Has anotha nigga been in here?" I looked at the messed-up bed, at towels on the floor, everything looked suspect.

"I swear, Rasheed, no one was here. I'm not seein' anyone. I told you, I love you, baby. You are the best thang that's eva happened to me."

There were tears wellin' up in her eyes and I thought, *why get so upset? Calm down.* I was jus' with Michelle anyway, even if she was lyin', fuck it. *Now we even.*

I let go of her shoulders and pulled her toward me. I hugged her and inhaled, tryin'a detect cologne or anything masculine. My mind was semi at ease when all I could smell was that warm vanilla scent that was all her. Time for damage control.

"I'm sorry, baby, I be gettin' worked up ova nothin'. It's jus' hard fa me 'cause you so fuckin' fine an' I'm worried one of these younga, betta-lookin' niggas is gonna come snatch you up one day." I leaned down and kissed her softly on the lips. She poked her bottom lip out in a cute pout and then kissed me back. I already knew where this was gonna go if I didn't stop it, so I broke away from the kiss and placed my lips on her forehead.

"Let's go get this car, okay?"

The dealership was only a ten-minute drive from the hotel. Pullin' up, I saw a jet-black Impala with dark tint and chrome accents. It had a huge red ribbon tied 'round it. My boy Ro was good. We got outta the car and I walked Honey over to it. Her eyes were the size of saucers, and I could tell she wanted to ask me if this one was for her but didn't wanna seem overly anxious, or like she was aimin' too high.

"Dawg, how you been?" Ro called out as he walked toward us. Roman was a short, midnight-black, chubby li'l nigga. We used to call him Magilla Gorilla in school. Derrick was the one who realized he could be of use a few years back when a few major suppliers went down and it was next to impossible to move shit in or out of the area wit'out bein' flagged. I always did all the deals and Derrick always handled the product supply once we got it. He saw one of those trucks that carries cars to the dealerships and thought of Ro. This nigga was *always* on our dicks in school; tryin'a help with this, or askin' 'bout that. He's what I called a fairy-tale hustla, and we the closest he would eva get to actually doin' any real hustlin'. It was easy: I paid the overhead for Ro's dealerships and, in return, if we needed to move supply, we simply loaded up a truck with hot cars and shipped 'em over to a sister dealership where one of my boys would unload and hit the street. Nothin' to it.

"What up, black?" I reached out and shook his hand. "Dis is Honey, wifey." I smiled over Honey's head and gave Ro a wink. She was grinnin' from ear to ear, too excited to stand still. Ro looked at Honey like he just ate an entire double chocolate cake and she was a tall, ice-cold glass of milk. She'd had her suit dry cleaned at the hotel and was lookin' like a million.

"Hi, Mr. Ro, nice to meet you." Honey reached to shake Ro's hand and he grabbed it and placed a kiss on the backside.

"A'ight, Casanova, that's enough, nigga." I put my arm aroun' Honey's shoulders. "Let's get my baby the keys so she can get a feel fa her new whip."

While Ro went inside to get the keys, I decided to get Honey's opinion of the car—not that I needed it.

"Wha'chu think, baby, is it what you had in mind or betta?"

She had her face pressed up against the glass, lookin' at the interior. Her phone was buzzin' in her purse but she didn't budge a muscle. "Daddy, I ain't got words right now, I'm so fuckin' happy. Oh my gosh!"

It felt good to make her happy. My phone started vibratin'. It was Derrick.

"Whatup, daddy daycare, you good?" I could hear a lot of noise in the background.

"Rah, yo, this li'l nigga trill!" Derrick was laughin' in the phone. "He playin' the Xbox an' he lovin' it. I hit the club but they said you weren't there. I got a drop scheduled tomorrow A.M. I figure we need fresh prod' for the streets, but I ain't gonna be able to get it wit' the kid."

I actually forgot all about the li'l nigga. Ro was makin' his way toward me. "D, lemme think on it an' I'll hit you in a few, a'ight?" I hung up jus' as Ro handed Honey the keys. She looked at me to see if it was okay to take 'em and I nodded. That was all she needed. Honey unlocked the driver's side door and hopped in. I looked over the roof of the car at Ro.

"We good on that paperwork?" I was referrin' to the fifty pounds of coke hidden throughout compartments in the car.

"Yessuh, we square as bricks." I laughed at Ro attemptin' to talk hood.

"Nigga, bricks ain' square, they rectangle, a plain ol' yes woulda did jus' fine." I looked into the car. "Baby, I got some work to handle. How 'bout you drive ya'self home an' get whatever you need for the rest of the week an' meet me back at the hotel. Might as well work your shift so you can earn some gas money."

Honey was so caught up in the car she barely answered me. I needed to work somethin' out to cover this drop in the A.M., get back to Chelle before I fucked up again, an' somehow get back outta the house to see Honey at the telly later. I got into my car and headed home to surprise Michelle.

# Smooth Criminal

## 17

I couldn't help feelin' déjà vu as, once again, I pulled into an empty driveway.

"Okay, what the hell is goin' on roun' here?" My words went unanswered in the empty house. I walked into the kitchen. The lasagna was covered and sittin' on the stove, and a half-empty bottle of wine was sittin' on the counter. I pulled out my cell and speed dialed Michelle's number, listenin' to the entire chorus of "Love All Over Me" twice before her voice mail picked up. I tried one more time. No answer. A nigga wasn't even hungry anymore. I turned on the TV to see if any games were on and sat down in my leather recliner, starin' at the screen but not really seein' it. I texted Derrick to let him know I'd handle the drop, and asked him to call and check on Big Baby at the club. His reply was "word." He musta been ova there tryin'a childproof his bachelor pad or figure out how to cook SpaghettiOs.

Wheneva I couldn't think somethin' through, or I needed a moment of peace, a shower always helped me refocus. I poured a glass of Merlot thinkin' that lasagna was pro'ly on point 'cause Michelle'd used half a damn bottle in the sauce. I walked into the bathroom and started the shower. I called Honey while I sipped on my wine and waited on the water to get hot, but hung up before she could answer—she was pro'ly at work already.

I stood completely under the showerhead and let the hot water run through my hair and down my body. So, Danita had a kid and *I* needed to find his ass a home. He couldn't stay wit' D forever. Figured the first and best thing to do would be find the li'l nigga's daddy. How the fuck was I gonna do that? I didn't even know where to start lookin'.

Dee knew my drop rotations. She could testify 'gainst my whole operation, even drop me on a few bodies and close some unsolved cases. I was lost in my thoughts. So lost, I didn't hear the door open or hear Michelle slide in the shower behind me, similar to the way I'd slid in on her. Before I could turn or speak I heard her draw in a sharp breath. She was eye to eye with the passion marks on my neck and back.

I didn't have time to block the first slap that landed hard against the side of my face an' ear.

"Nigga, you said you were workin'. I let you fuckin' touch me an' you been fuckin' anotha bitch?"

Michelle was yellin' and a nigga ear was ringin'. I was tryin'a think extra fast. I turned to face her and grabbed her by the wrist.

"Yo, Chelle, calm the fu—" I sidestepped to avoid her knee. The bitch was tryin'a hit a nigga where it counts, and you know what they say: don't eva fight a nigga when he naked. Som'n 'bout that shit make a mufucka go ninja on ya ass, blockin' shit, weavin', and counter attackin'. The shower was too confined for me to fully defend myself and one of her wet wrists slipped from my grip. I caught anotha slap across my chin as I tried to maneuver out of the shower.

"Why, Rasheed? I can't believe I let you fuck me. Did you wear a condom; do you even know if that bitch was clean?" Michelle was livid.

I mean, a nigga done fucked up before but she ain't neva actually seen physical evidence or caught me out there. It'd always been hearsay.

"Baby, stop an' jus' listen to me for a sec." I looked her in the eyes and let go of one of her hands to grab a towel off the rack. I know it wasn't nothin' but a towel, but it still helped a nigga feel just a li'l more secure. My mind was spinnin' a thousand stories for my mouth to give her, but not one made any sense, and I damn sure couldn't tell her the truth. Honey wasn't worth me losin' my home, my family, the only woman who eva loved me jus' for me.

"Baby, I ain't wanna tell you 'cause I ain' wanna scare you. Somebody tryin'a kill me. I got attacked by some bitch in my office las' night." *Ladies an' gentlemen, this nigga is a genius.* Chelle's forehead creased and I felt a new storm comin'.

"Rasheed, do I fuckin' look like I'm stupid to you? A bitch came in yo' office an' clawed up yo' back an' . . ." She turned and stormed out of the bathroom. "Fuck this shit, Rasheed. I'm done." She was in the bedroom tryin' to pull her jeans up over her wet skin.

"Michelle, where you goin'? I ain't lyin' to you!" Michelle paused long enough to grab the alarm clock off the dresser and hurl it in my direction.

"Nigga, jus' stop talkin' to me!" she yelled at me through her tears.

All the noise musta scared Trey, who started cryin' in his room. Michelle pushed past me. I followed her to Trey's room and stood in the door while she picked him up and kissed his tears, tellin' him it was okay even though she was still cryin' herself. It felt like this was gonna be the end of us. I looked at my "should be" wife holdin' the "would be" heir to everything I owned, and felt my eyes get hot as tears slid down my face.

"Chelle, please," I whispered, too choked up to really talk. "I ain' lyin', baby. I swear on my life." She looked at me with one eyebrow raised. Michelle ain' neva seen me cry. I had her attention.

"This crazy bitc . . ." I censored myself in front of Trey. "Crazy crack ho snuck a gun through security an' came at me in my office. I knocked the gun away from her but she still tried to fight me an' I hit her. I thought I knocked her out an' when I turned to get help she jumped on me, the crazy bitc . . . heffa damn bit me! We knocked over some product durin' the scuffle an' when she went for it I went to get D."

Michelle didn't say a word. She sat on the side of Trey's bed and laid him back down.

"Chelle, you know I wouldn't lie to you 'bout som'n like this. I been worried 'bout it ever since. Why you think it bothers me so much when you go runnin' 'round in the middle of the night alone?"

Trey was calm and already dozin' back off. I followed Michelle out of his room and back into our bedroom. Michelle sat on the edge of our bed and stared down at the floor. She looked nothing like the defiant, spirited woman I'd fallen in love with. She looked small, worn down. Defeated.

"I left to bring you some food since you were s'posed to be workin'. Derrick got your plate since you weren't there. He slipped up and mentioned what happened and told me you were lyin' low." Michelle started cryin' again. "I didn't know she hurt you. You looked fine, you were actin' fine. You shoulda said somethin' to me about it."

I froze in place. Michelle didn't notice my fists clench at my sides or see me grindin' my teeth.

She kept talkin'. "Yeah, I'm scared but, Rasheed, I deserve to know when my family is in danger."

Her last sentence fell on deaf ears. Derrick told her about the crack bitch? Derrick got my plate? I'd talked to Derrick and I knew for a fact Derrick wasn't at the club tonight; he was home with the kid. Why was she lyin' and who was she lyin' for? Shit, was Michelle at Derrick's place?

I forced myself to relax. Whateva the fuck was goin' on 'tween Michelle and my best friend/business partner would come to light. Give a nigga enough rope and if he smart he'll pull himself outta the hole he diggin', but if he ain't—he'll hang himself. I walked to the side of the bed and sat beside Michelle, takin' her hand into mine. I couldn't look her in the eye.

My hand was shakin'. I felt so gotdamn angry, I wanted to tear down the fuckin' walls. Michelle mistook my shakiness for fear and tried to console me.

"Rasheed, baby, we gonna get through this. It's gonna be okay, I promise."

She leaned over to hug me, and I felt betrayed, hurt, angry. My mouth was suddenly dry and my heart was flyin' in my chest. I couldn't even think clearly. I needed to lie down, close my eyes, and gather my thoughts.

# Who Does the Devil Trust

## 18

I couldn't sleep. Michelle lay beside me, snorin' softly, snuggled into my side. I stared at the ceiling and curled my lip in disgust, picturin' her snuggled up with my boy. I saw her in the shower, eyes closed, water drippin' off her skin. I couldn't help wonderin' if D seen her like that. It was startin' to make sense. How shook he was that night I came into the office through the back door, that same night Michelle had been blowin' up my phone. Events were playin' back in my mind. When I checked my texts he had asked if I was home. When I got home Michelle wasn't there that night. She woke me up and they were both at the house together. Had they just returned from a hotel, maybe he told her about Red before she came in to wake me up? I shook my head. Michelle woulda said somethin' sooner if she knew then.

A million and one questions ran through my mind. I could only come to one conclusion: they were seein' each otha, and it wouldn't be long before they tried to take me outta the equation all together. In the event somethin' happened to me I'd named Derrick as the overseer of everything I had until Trey turned eighteen. Now, I couldn't trust him. I'd made up my mind to change all my paperwork.

I couldn't blame Michelle for seekin' out anotha nigga. Afta everything I'd put her through I pretty much expected that shit to eventually happen, but D was my boy. He shoulda known betta. The world I functioned in was callous and cutthroat. If word got out that I let a nigga get away with somethin' as extreme as this it would be the end of my ass for certain. Every nigga on the East Coast would eventually try to cross swords with me. He left me with no choice. I needed to set an example.

Sometime durin' the endless tossin' and turnin', I'd finally fallen asleep. "Daddy, Daddy, up."

I smiled and opened my eyes. "Hey, li'l man." I grabbed Trey up from the side of the bed and growled, pullin' him under the covers. I found myself laughin' at his squeals and giggles while I tickled his sides.

"Why don't my two favorite men stop makin' all that noise and come get some blueberry pancakes?"

Michelle was standin' in the door, oven mitt on one hand, wearin' one of my old T-shirts. It hung down jus' above her knees and I could see the peaks of her nipples pokin' through the fabric. She smiled at me. Homeboy or no homeboy I could see why D pro'ly didn't honor the unspoken rule. Her jet-black hair hung loose down her back jus' past her shoulders, and even without makeup her skin looked flawless. She reminded me of Sanaa Lathan.

Trey hopped out of the bed and she scooped him up, plantin' kisses all over his face. "Let's go eat before greedy Daddy comes and gobbles up all the food."

I walked behind them into the kitchen and poured myself a glass of juice.

"How you feelin' today, baby?" Michelle was lookin' at me curiously.

"I'm good, but I got a small problem." I'd already made up my mind there was one small thing left to handle, and then I would try to win my baby back. But in the meantime I was gonna have to fully consider gettin' rid of my right-hand man. Back in the day Chelle used to do all the runs an' she'd actually picked up our las' drop due to another schedulin' conflict.

"I'ma need you to pick up another drop for me. D got some biz to handle."

"Rah, you said last time would be *the last time*. I'm getting too old for this type of shit. We need to sit down and have a serious talk about our future."

I didn't know if she was sincere, or if she was tryin' to find a way out of goin' because she knew it was a trap.

"Look, baby, jus' do this one last pickup please. I can't risk bein' followed by whoever it is tryin'a get at me right now. I swear I'll make it up to you." I didn't have to explain to her how a dead drop worked. All she had to do was take a cab to the Walmart over on Diven Street. I had the plate number for a silver Ford F-150 pickup parked in the eighth row. The doors would be unlocked and the keys were under the driver side floor mat.

I wasn't sure if I could trust Michele or Derrick at this point. If she got the car safely to my high rise on the other side of town she could park it in the garage and switch up. I had a Benz that was always parked there, unlocked, with a spare key taped under the back bumper. The entire thing shouldn't take more than an hour. Michelle nodded, no hesitation, and no questions asked otha than would I watch Trey 'til she got back? I picked him up and sat him at the table.

"We gonna eat us some pancakes an' watch cartoons. We'll be fine." Michelle walked over and kissed me on the cheek before headin' down the hall to shower and change. I still wasn't sure if I would eva be able to forgive her, but I was man enough to admit her li'l fling was my own fuckin' fault so I needed to live with it or move on.

I grabbed my phone off the charger and saw a text from Honey. *Shit! I completely forgot 'bout gettin' back to the hotel las' night. I'm sure she wouldn't mind me gettin' tied up jus' this once. Ain't like I didn't jus' buy—more like loan—her ass a car.* I decided to send her a text: "good morning sweetness." It didn't take long before she replied, "good morn' daddy I missed u - where were u, wut happnd?" I didn't answer her. I didn't feel like I needed to explain myself. Honey was in pocket and she won't a priority 'til I got Michelle *back* in pocket. I sat down at the table with my son and ate breakfast. My phone buzzed on the tabletop. "Ok, So wut happnd?" It was Honey again. I responded just to get her to stop textin' until Chelle left the house. "Work happened. Will hit u latr."

After Michelle left I hit Big Baby to get the numbers from las' night.

He answered his cell soundin' half asleep. "Yo, Rah, my nigga, what's good?" He yawned loud as hell in my ear.

"Damn, nigga, you still in the bed? What did we close at las' night?" He didn't immediately answer and I was about to repeat myself, but I heard a woman in the background.

"Big daddy, why da fuck you on da phone so early? Roll back ova hea' an . . ."

No, this nigga didn't. "Nigga? Is that Shiree? Are you for real fuckin' laid up right now?" I yelled into the phone. I ain't even need an answer.

The nigga started stutterin' and fumblin' the phone.

I hung up. That was the main reason I ain't neva let his ass run anything. He ain't had my numbers and he pro'ly used his li'l status for the night to fuck and cut deals with all the bitches. I shook my head. Unlike Derrick, at least Big knew his fuckin' place and wasn't tryin'a fuck *my* bitch. I didn't give a damn about him fuckin' Shiree. It jus' wasn't good business to have ere bitch tryin'a fuck whoeva was in charge for favors.

I lay on the couch to watch TV and fell asleep. Trey was lyin' on my chest with his thumb in his mouth, knocked out. It'd been almost four hours since Chelle left to pick up the drop. I was thinkin' the worst. Derrick pro'ly set me up and planned on me goin' when he said he couldn't, and I'd sent Michelle in my place. I couldn't call or text her. If she did get picked up, eventually they would run the phone records and nothin' needed to link back to me sendin' her out there. I had no choice but to wait. Honey was blowin' me up. I shoulda felt bad for standin' her up, but she wasn't givin' a nigga time to breathe. I finally broke down and sent her a text tellin' her shit was gettin' kinda heated on the streets and I was gonna lie low for a minute.

"You want me to come lie low wi'chu?"

I chuckled. Honey was always down for a nigga. That shit felt good, but I needed a break. "Nah, ma this shit jus' too crazy rite now. Niggaz want my head an' I cant risk puttin' u in danger." Wit' Honey in line, I could take time to get Michelle back in pocket. Maybe take a quick trip outta town. My phone lit up; it was Michelle.

"Hey, baby, everything good?" I was ready for anything.

"Yeah, we good. Caught a flat and thankfully I got help from some guy passin' by. I'm on my way home."

I smiled into the phone. My girl was on point. Yeah, it was definitely time we took a vacation. "While I'm thinkin' 'bout it, can you take a week or two off work, see if your moms can keep Trey? I gotta surprise." There was a brief pause. I was expectin' her to jump at the offer. *Don't tell me she caught up on that nigga.*

"Sure, Rasheed. I've been trainin' an intern. I'm sure she can run the numbers and keep my appointments for me while I'm away. She can almost run the place by herself."

*Whew.* I closed my eyes and unclenched my fist. For a sec I thought she was worried 'bout missin' Derrick, but she was jus' concerned 'bout her desk. "All right, baby, I'll see you when you get home. I got some calls to make. You gonna love it, I promise."

I needed to get a rotation worked out for the new shipment we jus' got in and get someone to cover the club and run the counts. D was always my first choice but now I had to consider otha options. I jus' couldn't trust him wit' my biz anymore. I called the only otha nigga besides Derrick I could trust.

"Big, you ready to work yet, or you still playin' in Shiree ass?" Big Baby was a fuck up, no doubt. But aside from fuckin' the strippers and drinkin' himself stupid at the bar, I knew he wouldn't touch my paper.

"Rah, my nig. Yo, I'm ready. Hope you ain' salty 'bout Shiree. You know how a nigga get off dat mufuckin' Cîroc. Big Shirley was callin' a nigga name!"

We laughed. "Yeah, nigga. I done heard her whisper 'Rah' a few times when I walked past my damn self. You good, jus' don't let that shit fuck up ya game. Need to fill you in on some serious shit, an' I need you to focus." I slid Trey off my chest onto the couch, and got up to go in the kitchen. I ran down the events of the las' couple of days up to the drop today. The other end of the line was completely silent. Big Baby was speechless.

"Big, it's cool—I'm cool. You know I would have both they mufuckin' heads, but I'm man enough to admit I really fucked up wit' Chelle."

Big took a long breath. "Rah, you my dude. I ain't know. I swear. There been a few times I seen Michelle up at the club. Early hours, though, before we opened. She'd come in, grab ya boy, and they go outside. I ain't think shit 'bout it. He always came right back so I jus' figured you sent her up there to pick som'n up or drop som'n off. I swear I woulda said som'n if I knew, Rah."

My throat tightened up, my mouth was dry. *How the fuck long this shit been goin' on?* All the fightin', all the arguin' ova what I was doin' and she was doin' her own dirt. I managed to croak out Big's instructions.

"Like I said, B, I got this one. Keep the club in line, run the counts, an' *now* you know so watch that nigga. Make sure the new product goes out. Any old shit that's left, trash it. Hit the streets, let 'em know them ODs was 'cause our shit *extra* right. We gonna make that shit profitable. I got new packages wit' new labels. We pushin' *Inferno* now, gonna be like fire in they veins, an' if they do too much I hope they right wit' *God* or they gonna witness the real thing." With that I hung up and pulled out one of the kitchen barstools to sit down.

I called to check Michelle's account, the one Honey set up. I wanted to make sure the six grand I used to open it was still there. I was gonna have Big do a few deposits from the club so I could start movin' the revenue from Inferno into one of my own accounts. I was gonna have to play nice with Michelle. The house was in her name, the cars were in her name, and there was also my son to consider. If she wanted to fuck me ova, she had a lot of ground. She made enough so erething looked legit. I honestly needed her a li'l more than I wanted to.

I was now a man on a mission. I desperately needed to win back my girl. She'd always wanted to go somewhere tropical and now seemed like the perfect opportunity to get her away from everything going on. I made a few phone calls and checked our passports. We both needed a vacation and I had every intention of making this one to remember.

# Lover's Paradise

# 19

I ran my toes through the white sand and looked at my watch. It was goin' on our second week in the Bahamas, and once again I was waiting for Chelle to finish a business call so we could go enjoy ourselves. I'd set us up at a seaside beach house. The shit cost retarded money but was worth it. From my understanding these super-rich white mufuckas buy these houses, fix 'em up, and pay who knows what in taxes jus' to live in 'em for a month or two at a time. They smart with it, though. When they ain't livin' in 'em they jus' rent 'em out and make you pay an ass load of paper. I shielded my eyes from the sun and looked up at the place. The walls were white stucco. I made a mental note when the caretaker was describin' shit to us. Niggas, I don't know what white stucco is, or what the hell it's made out of, but that shit's sexy! There were seven bedrooms all with heated tile floors and full baths. The master bedroom was on some *Scarface* shit! White carpet, white walls, Eastern king-sized bed. I ain't even know beds came bigga than king-sized.

One of the walls in the bedroom was jus' a row of glass doors that opened up to the beach. I could literally walk right outta those mufuckas, run a few steps, and dive into that ill-ass crystal blue water. Even with the ocean a few feet away we still had a rooftop pool, and that bitch looked like it jus' ran off the edge. Everything was beautiful. The palm trees, the bushes, all the tropical flowers. It was jus' my fuckin' luck Chelle started her cycle and, on top of that, her intern wasn't really workin' out. The girl was an idiot. She'd forgotten notes on half the shit Chelle told her, so the office was calling every five damn minutes. We were in paradise and she was too stressed to take care of a nigga, or enjoy herself. She'd already spent most of the trip glued to either her laptop or her cell phone. I was gettin' impatient.

The place was so big and empty sound traveled through it like nothin'. I could slightly make out Michelle's voice. It sounded like she was in the study. Oh, yes. That mufucka had a study, with bookshelves full of old, expensive, antique-lookin' books, some in English but most of 'em were Latin or French. Glass cases with all kindsa ol' white people artifacts like opera glasses, swords, and fabric somethin' eggs. Hell, I saw why I had to sign my life away and put down fifty thou as a deposit!

I turned the knob to walk into the study. It was locked. *What the hell?* I knocked an' could hear Michelle bustle toward the door.

"I'm so sorry, Rah, it must have locked by accident." She turned and went back toward the desk that was covered in what I guessed were contracts, and started typin' on her laptop.

"Well, are you ready to go grab some food? We need to call the caretaker an' get some more groceries delivered."

Chelle didn't even look in my direction. "I can't, Rah. I'm sorry. Cassidy is havin' a hard time negotiatin' this contract and she's too inexperienced to handle this big of a deal alone. I need to reconfigure these numbers and send it to her before she meets with the clients again tomorrow. I'll call the caretaker. Go get yourself somethin' to eat before it gets too late." She didn't miss a tap on that keyboard.

I walked out and closed the door. I jiggled the handle to make sure it didn't lock behind me.

I was glad my phone still worked out here. I was able to keep a heads-up on what was goin' on back home. Puttin' Big Baby in charge was actu-

ally a good move 'cause D was too busy playin'
daddy to do much of anything. Accordin' to Big,
Inferno was sellin' twice as fast as the usual
product. There was a concert, and afterward a
few big-time rappers and their entire entourage
came through and spent a lotta dough; the club
turned a week's worth of revenue in one night.
It was soundin' like erething was gettin' back to
normal. Erething, except for me and Michelle.
I'd told Honey I was leavin' town to lie low and
she understood. I texted her every so often, but
she was gettin' too inquisitive, too needy actin'. I
didn't know what happened to her li'l homegirls
but when I *needed* them to be distractin' her ass,
they weren't doin' it.

I'd decided to shower and shave before goin'
out to find myself somethin' for dinner. Even
with the sun goin' down it was still warm out. I
put on some white linen shorts and a matchin'
shirt that buttoned up, but said fuck it and
decided to leave the buttons undone and just
go barechested. My yella ass needed to get a
li'l tan anyway. Michelle was still barricaded
in the study, goin' ova numbers or whateva. I
didn't even bother tellin' her I was leavin'. The
beach house was gated and kind of secluded
so I walked down the beach, lost in thought. I
was about a mile away from the house when my

stomach growled and reminded me I was s'posed to be lookin' for food. I didn't even notice that it'd gotten dark out. I could hear drums and people laughin' somewhere up ahead; sounded like they were havin' a good-ass time, maybe they had a li'l bar or somethin' out here.

I'd followed the sound of the music all the way up to what I guessed was someone else's beach backyard. They had Tiki torches goin' and a bonfire. As I got closer, I could see it was a party or cookout of some kind and there were women all over the place. *Guess I'm crashin'*. I was glad I wore what I did; as I passed a few guys standin' by the fire I noticed ereone had on all white. My view was blocked by a line of trees, but as I walked aroun' the small forest that served as a privacy fence I woulda sworn I'd jus' died and this was heaven.

The house looked almost ten times bigger than the one me and Michelle were stayin' in. The sand traveled halfway up toward the house and then turned into white stone with a huge, dimly lit pool in the center. The pool was so damn big they put a small island in the middle of it, with trees and even what looked like a small cave. The entire back of the house had white columns that ran like some Greek shit I'd seen in a book when I was a kid. Everything 'bout that mufucka screamed money, like Oprah or Bill Gates money. I could start to see more people as I got closer. There were tables set out all over the place with white tea light candles and white flowers on 'em. A few tables were full, but no one really paid me any mind as I walked through and tilted my head in greetin' to the few people who did look my way. All I saw was black folk. I jus' knew this was someone famous, a ball player or a singer—somethin'.

A nigga's spider-senses were definitely tinglin'. I passed a couple of bitches in the pool kissin' and almost tripped ova my own feet. I was used to strippers, fat-assed, down the street, thick, everyday bitches. These were model, TV, half black an' somethin', titty job and Botox injection, exotic-lookin' bitches. There was a buffet table set up jus' before the steps leadin' into the house. I picked up a plate and grabbed myself some wings.

"What up, you eva been to one of these before?" I looked up; some dark-skinned nigga was pilin' up his plate on the other side of the buffet table, talkin' to me.

"Oh, yeah, nigga, shit nice, huh?" I answered, soundin' like I did this kinda shit ereday.

He looked aroun' and leaned like he ain't want anyone to hear him, even though there was no one within' a ten-foot radius.

"I bought the Empyrean package. The shit was a flat two hundred grand. I'm hopin' it's worth it. I ain't neva spent that much before."

I raised my eyebrows and nodded. "I'm sure you gonna have a good fuckin' time. I'm 'bout to head inside." I had no idea what he bought but I ain't wanna be an accomplice to a damn thang; sounded like product to me. I started eatin' my wings and walked into the mansion.

This was the kinda shit you see on TV. The first thing that caught my eye was what I thought was a statue of a woman. I walked toward it, admiring the glitterin' gold ass and was 'bout to admire some glitterin' gold titties until the mufucka looked at me. A nigga almost shot up outta there, chicken wings and bones trailin' behind all over the marble floor. I didn't even notice all the different metallic-hued statues when I came in. People were crowded aroun' a few here and there. I brought my eyes back to goldie. Her hands were palms together in front of her stomach, like she was prayin' standin' up. She looked back at me silently with the sexiest grey eyes. I heard someone walking past me say somethin' 'bout livin' statues, they completely naked 'cept the body paint. I had to start thinkin' 'bout baseball and doughnuts 'cause a nigga was 'bout to show goldie and anyone else who wanted to see that I was enjoyin' the display. They had a free bar set up on the side. I went over and ordered a shot of Remy, then ordered myself two more. I needed to relax.

I saw niggas who looked like they could be from 'round the corner or outta a movie. It was hard to tell who had paper and who didn't. The same went for the women. They were everywhere, some in white dresses, some in white skirts and tops, some in nothin' but bikini bottoms. I made my way through a crowd of people gathered aroun' what I thought was a *Soul Train* line or some people dancin'. I was tryin'a get closer to see what had everyone's attention. We were in the middle of a huge foyer an' the walls were all lined wit' pillars. There wasn't a single light on in the entire place. Candles were set up everywhere. I slowly pushed my way through the crowd to get a better look at whatever new performin' artist surprise had them starin' in silence. I'd jus' excused myself past a tall-ass nigga I swear coulda been a playa I know from the Suns, but immediately lost all thought as the movement in the center of the room finally caught my eye.

The floor was draped with red silk. I could smell jasmine and what I thought was weed. I found myself frozen in place watchin' as this lean

ebony-dark girl wit' long jet-black hair was lyin'
on her stomach. I had no idea if she was cute,
ugly, or what 'cause her face was buried in anotha bitch pussy. What the hell did I walk into?
The crowd was a mixture of men an' women. Everyone was watchin' and jus' enjoyin' the show.
I crossed my arms in front of me and acted like
I belonged. The bitch eatin' pussy stopped and
started to get up, while the other girl got on all
fours. I could feel myself gettin' excited. The
dark-skinned one was actually finer than a mufucka. As she got up I noticed she had thick, full
lips, big, round titties—nipples pointed—and . . .
What the fuck . . . The bitch had a dick! I had to
fight every muscle in my body to keep my composure. No one else seemed even the least bit
shocked. She was a he and she/he was postin' up
to fuck the otha bitch and that definitely was not
a strap-on!

I slowly eased my way outta the group jus' as
easily as I'd eased in. I was backin' my way toward the doors and I bumped into what I'd have
to say was one of the most beautiful women I'd
eva seen in my entire life. She was small, 'bout
five one, and she had the face a million bitches
would sell they souls to have.

"Damn, I didn't see you down there." I chuckled. Shit, I was actually nervous. For the first

time in my adult life, a *woman* was givin' me the jitters.

"Maybe you should pay more attention to where you stomp, Sasquatch."

She had a slight accent. I'm from the streets so if it ain't Spanish or Chinese I really can't place it, but it was sexy than a mufucka. "Wow, why so hostile? I apologized to you an' erethang." She was staring up at me angrily like a mini tigress ready to pounce. For a moment I jus' stared back and found myself amazed at how fuckin' beautiful she was. I couldn't tell if she was white, light-skinned, or what, and her eyes were a sexy golden-hued brown. A breeze was comin' in through the door behind her and her fragrance drifted into my senses. She smelled like sweet coconut and vanilla.

"Calm down, love, let me make it up to you. What's ya name?" What can I say? I'm jus' a charmin' mufucka. Her name was Leilani and I was in complete lust with her fine li'l petite ass. A human sculpture walked past. I did my best to ignore the fact that it was a naked green nigga, and grabbed two champagne glasses off his tray.

She took her glass and started to walk outside. I followed her like a puppy.

"How do you like it here so far? Have you played yet?"

I wasn't sure what she meant, but if what I saw inside was how these niggas played, I wasn't goin'.

"No, love, it's not really my scene. I'm even tempted to ask if you all woman from what I seen up in here tonight. What the fuck kinda party is this?" My cell phone buzzed in my pocket and I jumped. It was Chelle. I ignored the call. She'd been ignorin' my needs this whole trip and I needed to relieve some tension. I put my phone back into my pocket and waited for Leilani to answer my question.

We'd walked out of sight of the house opposite of the way I'd wandered in from the beach. There was a gazebo with torches set up 'round it. I could see dozens of pillows scattered 'round on the floor. I was gettin' even more excited and nervous as I followed her toward it. I gulped down the rest of my champagne and was relieved to see a bottle sittin' in an ice bucket inside. I picked it up and poured us fresh glasses, then sat down on what had to be the softest red and gold pillows I'd eva put my ass on.

"This is Hedonism. You probably shouldn't be here, but I like how you are different so I will not say anything." Her accent made her pronounce all of her words so fluently. I couldn't wait to see what she sounded like moanin' my name. I really didn't peg her as the screamin' type.

"Hedonism, ain' that some kinda Sodom-an'-Gomorrah-type shit?" I felt like a li'l kid again, all this shit was so new and so different.

"No, babee, you misunderstand the term. Hedonism is universal love and passion. There is no jealousy. No boundaries. People pay great amounts of money to participate here. There are no rules and there is no one to tell you that your desires are bad or wrong."

One word was swirlin' in my head as my eyes widened in understandin': *Jackpot!*

Turned out her husband ran the whole fuckin' thing. He even dipped and dabbled wit' men and women but ironically was too jealous to let Leilani do her thang and too involved to give her any attention. Over the course of the next two hours I fucked her in every position I could think of and some that would have never crossed my mind in this lifetime. I was in heaven, but I needed a quick break and reluctantly separated myself from Leilani's body. As I reclined against the pillows she took a sip from her glass and started suck a nigga dick with a mouthful of cold champagne.

"Love, jus' gimme a few minutes. I promise daddy got a lot more." I was close to bein' fucked up from all the shots and champagne on a pretty much empty stomach. This shit felt like a dream.

I was watchin' Leilani's lips while she worked me back into stiffness. I didn't see her husband watchin' us, I didn't hear him walk up on us. My head was leaned back and my eyes were closed. I felt a sharp, splittin' pain as I was hit across the back of the head and then it went black.

# The Greatest Man Alive

## 20

.It felt like my mouth was full of sand and I was burnin' up.

"Chelle, turn the AC on. Baby, it's hot." I thought I was home in my bed. I tried to open my eyes but the light was too bright and I felt a searing pain shoot across my face and temples. I managed to squint as best I could and was hit by a wave of nausea. I rolled onto my side and vomited 'til there was nothin' left but dry heaves. I was naked. The night before flooded back to me in one large flashback, up 'til the part where I was gettin' head an' then nothin'. *What the fuck did she do to me?* I could barely make out my linen shorts in the sand a few feet away. It hurt like hell to move but I needed to get the fuck outta there. I maneuvered into my shorts and was relieved my wallet and cell were still in 'em. I did my best to stand and began limpin' my way across the beach, prayin' that if God jus' got me back to the house I'd be a good nigga from now on.

I passed the colossal house that now looked cold and deserted. The party was over and ere-one had left to go back to their normal lives. It felt like forever but, finally, I could see the white stucco of the house we were stayin' in. That was all I needed. There was no energy left in my body and I collapsed by the bedroom doors that over-looked the beach. My ears were ringin' and my head was poundin'. No. My ears weren't ringin', it was a woman screamin' my name.

"Rasheed. Rasheed, baby, please open your eyes for me, look at me. What happened to you? Baby, please, open your eyes."

Michelle was kneelin' down beside me and her voice was slammin' 'round in my head, makin' it hurt even worse. Damn, a nigga felt like he was 'bout to be sick again.

"Please, lower your voice, you killin' me right now." Michelle was so happy I replied, she grabbed me in a tight hug, but quickly let me go when she realized how much pain I was in.

"Baby, what the hell happened to you?"

Somewhere during the painful trudge from the gazebo to our bedroom doors I'd figured out what happened. Leilani's jealous husband must have seen us, and I didn't know how she kept him from killin' me right there on the spot.

"Baby, I went to get somethin' to eat an' got jumped. They tried to rob me. I musta blacked out when someone hit me 'cross the head."

Ya boy deserved an Oscar. Chelle helped me up and into the house. She already knew not to even mention callin' the police. What's done is done when it comes to violence in the streets, or on the beach for that matta. You get caught sleepin' it's ya own damn fault. She helped me lie down on the bed and went to get me some water and a towel with ice in it.

"Rah, I was so mad at you, baby. I jus' knew you were up to no good. I prayed you would learn your lesson one day. I had no idea you were really in trouble. My poor baby." She started cryin' and did her best to wipe the dried blood off my head and neck. I closed my eyes and drifted off to sleep. I thought I smelled coconut vanilla and smiled. He mighta knocked me out, but I still got dat ass. And what a fine mufuckin' ass it was!

I spent the nex' three days in bed recuperatin' and Chelle finally put her job on hold to take care of me. Despite erething, the shit seemed to be workin' out in my favor. We only had a couple of nights left and Chelle decided we should try our best to enjoy 'em, and I agreed. We spent a lot of time talkin', jokin', and really becomin' friends again. I'd forgotten how much alike we were. We had the same sense of humor, liked the same kinda movies; hell, I'd even forgotten that we were both left-handed.

I was sittin' at the kitchen table, lost in my thoughts, watchin' Michelle work around the stove through the steam. Fresh garlic and olive oil scented the air and my stomach growled. I couldn't wait until that veal Parmesan hit my lips. My phone went off. It was a text from Honey.

> Hey, daddy, I'm really missin' u rite now.
> Big Baby been a big pain in da ass, wen u
> commn home?

I laughed and looked up at Chelle.

"Big Baby say he thinkin' 'bout marryin' Shiree!" She laughed. If I acted like I was talkin' to him she wouldn't pay me any mind. I texted Honey back.

> I miss u 2 baby. U keepin' it tite fa me or
> u out there givn it away?

She replied right back. Um keepin' it fa u. But dey sayin' u wit ya baby momma. I didn't know u had a baby momma or a baby. Dey lyin rite???

I sighed. I'd kept my family life as far from Honey for as long as I possibly could. I guessed it was time I told her wassup.

Yeah, luv, my bitch-ass baby momma here too. I don't like mufukaz to kno I got fam. I only got one son an even if his momma a asshole I gotta keep her stupid ass safe 2. Bein' stuck listnen to her dumb ass makin' me miss you so much. U don't evn kno. It's a big house tho. I stay in my part an' she stay in hers.

I didn't get an immediate reply like I normally did. I got up to go relieve myself and walked out of the kitchen toward the study.

"Where you goin', baby? Dinner's ready." Chelle was fixin' my plate, lookin' extra right in a snug pink sundress.

"Be right back, gotta take a leak." She moved toward me as if she thought I might need help. "Damn, woman, I'm not gonna fall in. I'll be okay, I promise." I didn't mean to snap at her. But damn. I needed to feel like myself again. I needed to feel in charge.

A soft humming sound caught my attention as I walked past the cracked door of the study. Chelle's BlackBerry was lying on the desk next to her laptop, vibratin' and threatenin' to shake itself right onto the hardwood floor. I couldn't help myself. As much as I hated it when women went through my shit, I needed to see who she'd been talking to so much. I tapped the screen, momentarily forgetting that it wasn't like my own touch screen phone, and found myself feelin' clumsy and awkward handling her petite pink phone.

The trackball lit up and I scrolled to her message box. "1 new text D." I immediately recognized Derrick's number. A dull thud started in my temple that painfully throbbed in tune with my speedin' heart. I clicked on the envelope.

Take all the time you need sweetheart. I'll be here whenever you need it.

Michelle had been deleting her messages so I couldn't find whatever it was she sent to make Derrick reply. What the fuck did she say to him? Sweetheart? Why the fuck wasn't he backin' down? My appetite was gone. I deleted the message and put the phone back where I'd found it. I needed to compose myself quick. My palms were cold and clammy and the pain in my head was so intense I was squinting. I splashed cold water over my face and stared at my reflection in the mirror. *What's done is done, an example would be made.*

"Smells good, baby. Come feed big daddy an' later big daddy gonna feed you." I planted a false smile on my face as I strolled to the table and took my seat.

"Five more seconds and I was gonna come lookin' for you. Glad you made it back."

Michelle smiled and pressed a warm, soft kiss against my forehead as she set my plate down in front of me. I picked my phone up from where I'd left it and secretly chastised myself for leavin' it unlocked. I locked my phone and put it away.

I was finally feelin' like myself and after dinner, while Michelle cleared the dishes, I went into the bedroom and drew a bubble bath. I poured honey in the water and dropped in a few fresh peach slices I'd found sittin' in the fridge. Don't get it twisted, this nigga knew how to get romantic. Bitches love this shit; any nigga who like pussy as much as I did gotta fuckin' PhD in how to get panties off. I grabbed some petals off a bright orange somethin' outside the bedroom door and prayed the damn thing wasn't poisonous as I dropped 'em in the tub. Chelle was in the kitchen, washin' the dishes. I walked in and hugged her from behind, scarin' her outta whateva daydream she was in. She jumped and dropped a plate in the sink, splashin' dishwater on us both.

"Rasheed!"

"Damn, baby, you act like the boogieman got chu or som'n. You wouldn't scare so easy if you weren't so bad all the time. Come take a bath wit' me."

We hadn't shared a bath together since before Trey was born. I ain't had a taste for Remy or champagne since the night at the mansion, so I'd made margaritas and set 'em beside the tub. Chelle let her hair hang loose the way I liked it, and walked naked into the bathroom. I admired her as she got in the tub. She was kinda like a tall milk-chocolate Amazonian version of Leilani. I was definitely one lucky mufucka. We were lyin' back in the tub, soakin' in the fragrant water. Chelle was sittin' between my legs with her back against my chest, head under my chin, eyes closed. Her hand was under the water, drawing lazy patterns on my skin that stretched sensually from my calf up to my thigh, when suddenly she stopped.

"Rah, I been meanin' to ask you som'n 'bout the other night, but wanted to wait 'til you were better."

My mind started racin' and my heart sped up, but on the outside I showed no signs of worry. I kissed the top of her head and took a sip from my margarita. "Wassup, baby, ask me?" Chelle took a deep breath. I already knew this was gonna be an earful.

"Well, the night you got jumped, you said they were tryin' a rob you. But when I undressed you, your phone and wallet were in your pocket. None of your credit cards were missin'. It didn't look like you'd even lost any money."

My guilty subconscious wanted to whisper the truth but my mind was screaming, *think, nigga, think.*

"I don't understand how you were assaulted an' knocked unconscious but they didn't take shit off you. An' you had a number written on a napkin. No name, jus' a number wit' the word 'Hedonism' written underneath."

I know she had to feel my heart beatin'. *Leilani left me her number!* She musta snuck out and put it in my shorts before they left the mansion. Damn, I needed that number.

"It's still fuzzy, Chelle. I think I'd found a bar an' had a drink. The bartender told me the name of a club in the area. I wanted to see how the competition out here looked. Maybe send Big Baby back to open up another spot. It's real vague. I remember walkin' down the beach an' passin' some kids. I remember the same kids were still there when I was makin' my way back home. I passed 'em an' the only other thing I remember is I felt my head explode in pain. Maybe someone spooked 'em before they could take my shit. There was a party a few houses down." I relaxed. *I am the world's greatest nigga! I could sell sand in a desert! Hell, I could sell pork to a Muslim if I wanted to!* Chelle seemed to accept my answer and leaned back.

"Well I'm glad you're okay, baby. Thank God for angels."

I smiled to myself. I was thankin' Him too, for li'l exotic coconut-vanilla-smellin' angels with pouty dick-suckin' lips.

"I still wanna check out that club. Did you throw away the napkin?" I held my breath.

"Of course I did. I didn't know if you were into some shit. I didn't think we needed anything in the house to link you back to any trouble." I slowly exhaled. *Oh well, so much for that.* Short of diggin' through the trash there was no way for me to reconnect with Leilani. I made a mental note to start askin' some of my more connected clients about the kind of parties Leilani and her husband catered to. There had to be an easy way to find that woman again.

# Three's A Crowd

## 21

We had a peaceful flight back to the states, first class of course. A nigga was feelin' ready to take on the world. I hadn't heard much from my boy D while we were gone. I had Big Baby give ereone explicit instructions on keepin' contact to a minimum with me. He did send me a text lettin' me know the prod' was almost completely sold out. They were 'bout to process the last two cases from the shipment and it was time to order more. Other than that, erething was peaceful. Honey even hit me sayin' she undastood and was cool with me takin' my baby momma into hidin' while shit cooled off. She ain't had her "crack" in a minute. I needed to see her soon or it would only be a matter of time before she started trippin'.

We stopped and picked Trey up on our way home from the airport. My li'l boy was getting big, and lookin' more and more like me by the day. His hair was even goin' from that straight, white-boy-lookin' shit and it was finally gettin' a li'l curl to it like mine. Yeah, we got that good shit! It was midafternoon and Chelle had been desperate to get back to the office e'er since we landed.

"Go 'head, girl. I'll chill wit' Trey an' unpack. It's cool." I wasn't ready to get back to my street life jus' yet anyway.

"Thank you, Rah. The trip was beautiful, baby, thank you so much." She kissed me and hopped into her car.

"I'll be home as soon as I get all the details on the contract squared away." I worried 'bout her lyin' and leavin' me to see Derrick, so I texted Big and asked him to get up wit' the nigga and go over plans or somethin' to see if he declined or accepted. I texted Honey too.

Daddy's Home! I wanna see you tonite.

I took Trey inside and brought in the luggage. It really felt good to be back home. I sat him down, ordered a pizza, and turned on his favorite *SpongeBob* DVD so I could start unpackin' our clothes. Three hours and too many damn bags that weren't even mine later, I was done. I was too tired to give Trey a bath so I jus' stood him in the shower with me and washed him up. We were pj'd up, and before I knew it, dozin' on the couch.

Nightfall crept up on my ass. It seemed like I'd only closed my eyes for a second. I felt panic when I realized Trey wasn't lyin' on my chest. I jumped up and ran down the hall to check his bedroom. He was all tucked in and sound asleep. Michelle must have come home and laid him down, but why didn't she wake me up? My phone was buzzin' somewhere in the livin' room, but I couldn't' remember where I'd laid it and didn't see it in any of its usual places. I followed the sound and located it on the floor beside the couch. *Musta fell when I was asleep*. I unlocked it.

Honey had replied.

I'll be at the hotel daddy. Meet me after my shift.

It was only eleven. I still had an hour before she got off. I went into the bedroom to tell Michelle I was leavin', but she was knocked out and snorin' softly into her pillow, so I jus' changed into some jeans, threw on a T-shirt, and headed out the door.

I got to room 145 as usual and decided to rub one out before Honey got there. I needed to wear her ass the fuck out, remind her exactly who her nigga was. I ain't had the patience for all the questionin' and textin' me all the time. Yeah, one good dick-down would solve all that shit. I flipped through the hotel's On Demand menu, passin' skinny white girls with huge balloon titties and Botox lips before finally deciding on one of the only ones they were showin' that featured black folk. Before I could even get started, my phone went off. It was Big Baby. The only reason I even answered was because I was certain he might have some info on D.

"B, talk to me." I held my breath.

"Whatup, Rah, bad news. Mufuckin' fiends OD'n all ova the fuckin' place. The news is lit the fuck up talkin' 'bout mufuckas in the ER." I let out a sigh of relief and disappointment, still unsure on how I felt about my boy Derrick and all the shadiness. Big continued but I was only half listening to him.

"More than a few of 'em had Inferno packs when they got picked up."

"Well, damn. It's a good thang that shit's new new. It'll take 'em a minute to figure out who distributin' since we switched up our packagin'. Glad I thought of that shit! I jus' don't need no mufuckas rattin' out they sources an' gettin' my boys locked up tho', fuck!"

"Yo, Rah, it's funny we always get our shipments offa Derrick's connect. I'm thinkin' the nigga might be tryin'a set you up." This nigga read my mufuckin' mind.

"B, I'm thinkin' the same thing an' it might be time we handled this seriously." There was a knock on the door; it had to be Honey.

"Yo, I'ma hit you in the A.M. an' we gon' finish this convo."

I opened the door and took in the vision standin' in the hallway. Gotdamn she was thick. Honey didn't even bother changin' after her show. She threw a trench coat on and drove her ass over here like that jus' for me. A nigga was feelin' good again.

"Hey, daddy, you gon' let me in or you gon' stand there an' let ya pussy get cold?"

Damn I loved that li'l ghetto baby voice.

"I missed you, girl. Get ya thick ass in here." I pulled Honey in the room, yankin' the trench coat down off her body. Either she'd gotten thicker or a nigga memory was gettin' lax. I got down on my knees, and said a silent thank you—she had on crotchless panties.

"Baby, what chu doin'?" She looked down at me, curiosity written all over her face.

"You'll see."

I kissed her just above her belly button, and then let my lips slide down her stomach. I kissed all the way down until I reached the area where the panties gapped open and there was nothin' but wet pussy. Honey had her fingers in my hair and had closed her eyes. I leaned her back against the door and placed her leg over my shoulder. I used my tongue to separate her moist, hot center and massaged soft circles 'round her clit. I didn't get a chance to pre-game so I needed to get her off quick. I increased the pressure and knew I was doin' it right when Honey's fingers tightened almost painfully in my hair as she moaned my name, lost in what I was doin' to her. She tasted good. I'd never eatin' her pussy before and was surprised that she was so sweet. It was like strawberries and chicken. I was trippin'.

"I can't, baby. Oh fuck. Please stop," Honey half moaned and half whined, but I knew what she meant. She didn't think she could cum standin' up. I concentrated and put even more pressure on her clit while reachin' up to play with her nipple through the thin fabric of her lingerie. She was 'bout to let go and I was ready. In one smooth motion I picked her up, walked over, and laid her on the bed. I got on my knees beside the bed, put one of her legs on each shoulder, and went back to work while undoin' my pants. Honey tasted jus' like honey as I felt her legs tense and start to shake on my shoulders. I quickly got up and positioned myself. I slid in hard and deep just as she climaxed. Honey screamed my name and I started countin' basketballs in my head.

There was no comparin' Honey's pussy to any otha bitch's pussy—eva. She was so confident in her skin, I could get off jus' from watchin' her. She had her head thrown back and her fingers were busy playin' with her nipples one minute, and then she'd be lookin' me in the eye tellin' me how much she loved this dick the next. I couldn't take it. Too many nights of pullin' out and fin-ishin' myself off made me crave this shit. I laid my body down on hers and cupped her ass so I could go deeper. I decided to try somethin' new and slid one of my fingers into Honey's ass jus' to see if she'd like it.

"Oh. My. Damn. Nigga!" She came again and that was it, her pussy was pullin' me in and I couldn't fight back.

"Fuck, baby, I'm 'bout to . . ." Before I could get the words out I felt myself explode.

Somewhere in the room a bee was buzzin' or a . . . I looked up. My phone had fallen out of my pants and was vibratin' on the floor. I looked at the clock and my heart jumped in my chest. *Fuck!* It was six A.M. Honey was underneath me, still asleep. I already knew it was Michelle and she was most likely pissed. My plan was to come here, dick Honey down, then shower and leave. I didn't know what the fuck happened. I hopped up and started gettin' dressed like my ass was on fire.

"You goin' to get us breakfast, daddy?" Honey was half asleep. She rolled onto her side, turning her back to me.

"Nah, baby, I'm s'posed to pick my son up from his grandma house and take him to daycare. I gotta go but I'll come back, okay?" I looked to see if she was upset or about to fuss, but Honey was almost asleep.

"Okay, baby, call me when you on the way."

I drove like a madman, mind shootin' over a hundred and one things I could tell Chelle, but none of 'em were gonna work. Not this time. I was angry at myself, but I was more angry at Michelle. If she would jus' try with a nigga sometimes, maybe I wouldn't have to get pussy elsewhere. Honey did my ass right and the shit put me out cold for the night. Maybe if Chelle woulda jus' *tried* to be down for whateva, be a li'l creative, or experiment, our shit wouldn't be so fucked up. I pulled up at six twenty-eight and immediately felt my stomach sink in disappointment. Once again I'd spent the night away from home, and Michelle had already left for work, so there was no downplayin' my absence.

# Lights Out

## 22

I called Michelle's cell and went straight to voice mail. I'd fucked up. I wasn't even in the mood to go back to the hotel so I decided to go count the safe at the club and make sure the place was still standin'. I needed to figure out how to deal wit' D and this whole bad-product situation, too. I wasn't sure what I'd do with Danita's son, but I'd have to find him another place to stay. My mind was heavy with questions, decisions, and doubt. I didn't expect anyone to be at the club at this hour, but Big Baby's car was parked outside. I found him sleepin' in my office on the couch.

"Nigga." I tapped his leg. "What the hell you doin' in here?" Big Baby was almost two times larger than the couch, so his neck was bent at a crazy angle and his feet were hanging over the end. There was no way he could've been comfortable.

"Damn, Rah, I ain't expect to see you. What up, boy?" He sat up and dapped me up. "Yo, word got back to my ol' lady that I was fuckin' 'roun' wit' Shiree. She flipped da fuck out. Put me out an' then hit Shiree an' put a nigga on blast." Big Baby looked down at the floor like a lost puppy. "I ain't have nowhere else to go."

I wasn't surprised. Big Baby could neva do dirt and not get caught, but as always, once the groceries got low or the light bill needed payin', his ol' lady would take him back and they'd be fine.

"It's cool, B. Stay as long as you need. Jus' don't clog up my fuckin' toilet. I'ma go run a count on the safes."

I could see him breathe a visible sigh of relief as he shuffled himself back down into that ungodly uncomfortable position. I cleared all the safes and was pleased with the money they'd been pullin' in while I was away. I was a li'l surprised when I got to Honey's and there was no cash inside. We were definitely gonna have words. I went back into my office to lock everything up in my safe. I'd count it later. I entered the code and opened the door. The ATM card reminded me of the day I took Honey to the bank. I'd never watched the surveillance from that day. Big was snorin' loudly on the couch, dead to the world. I needed to catch up on what'd been goin' on. I slid into my desk and logged on to my computer to pull up the camera footage.

Everything looked normal. It was 3:00 P.M. Derrick came in and checked the bar and register. He was walkin' aroun' makin' sure the stage was clear and the lights worked. I was 'bout to fast forward it, and reached for the mouse. Big Baby started talkin' and I looked away from the video to see if he was gonna come over, but he was jus' talkin' in his sleep. I chuckled. A nigga who talks in his sleep is a nigga who'll tell on himself. I looked back at the video, intent on fast forwarding to something worth watching, when my hand paused mid-motion. Derrick was on the phone by the bar. He had started pacin' back and forth, slashin' his hand through the air. It was obvious he wasn't too pleased about something. I would have paid anything for sound. He slammed down the phone and sat at the bar, looking defeated. Was that his connect he was talking to? Maybe it was Michelle. I didn't have long to wonder. As if on cue Michelle walked into the frame on the surveillance.

I remembered this day. The outfit she had on was what she wore to work the day that I came home and told her we were goin' out to dinner. She walked up to Derrick and put her arms around his shoulders. Without sound I had no idea what was being said. She looked happy to see him and my heart pounded in my ears as if it were shouting the word "betrayal" over and over. She was talkin' into his ear, too close for my comfort. Derrick stood and shook his head yes and they hugged again before walking out.

I started breathin' again. I watched that scene ten times. They seemed too casual, too familiar with each other. I imagined a hundred and one scenarios and not one made me feel any better. They must have had plans that night, and she called to tell him she couldn't go and he was upset so she showed up to smooth it over in person. Maybe she was tryin' to break it off wit' him. It was one thing thinkin' of them together, but seein' them made me feel a new type of anger. Not only had Michelle spoken the words outta her fuckin' mouth, but now I had physical evidence of them together.

"Big, get the fuck up!" I stopped the video and went into my safe, pullin' out fifty grand.

"Wh . . . what, ni . . . nigga?" Big was sittin' up in a confused daze.

I shoved the cash into his hand. "Take care of our *problem* for good, nigga." I looked him in the eye and he mouthed Derrick's name. I was goin' back to the hotel. I needed to lie down. I needed to be calm again before I saw Michelle. I had forgiven her, but seein' that shit drove a nigga damn

near insane. I wasn't sure how she'd take it wheneva she got the news that the nigga was ghost,
but her li'l love triangle was dead. Literally.

I took the long way to the hotel; I needed to
calm the fuck down. I would just surprise Honey
so I didn't bother textin' to let her know I was
on my way. As I neared the turn to pull into the
hotel parkin' lot I could see all the lights before
I could see the commotion. There were cop cars
all ova the fuckin' place. I passed the turn and
looked as best as I could without seemin' suspicious. I almost crashed into a truck stopped at
the light on the corner when I saw Honey bein'
led out, head down and hands behind her back.
They at least had the decency to let her wear her
coat out. She looked so small and pitiful as she
climbed into the back of a car. I was determined
to get to the safest place I could think of: my safe
house.

No one—not Derrick, not Michelle, Big Baby,
hell, not even Honey—knew 'bout the spot I'd
bought in a quiet suburban neighborhood just
outside of Chesapeake near Pungo. Most of the
people kept to themselves and didn't care if
anyone lived in the house or not. They pro'ly jus'
assumed I was military and stayed deployed a

lot. Either way, if anyone tried to rat me out, I knew this was the last place anyone would look. I pulled up in front of the ranch-style brick house with its mint-green shutters and overgrown lawn. I opened the garage, pulled my car inside, and went into the house.

The place had the bare essentials. The lights and water bill weren't even in my name. I'd paid a helluva deposit to get the services with no Social Security number and had even had the foresight to give a fake name. I paid the bill on-line with a credit card I loaded up with cash, so nothin' connected me or the club. It was a small two-bedroom house with nothin' but a couch, small TV, and a bed in the larger of the two small rooms. As I opened the hall closet, I was relieved my gun safe was locked and looked secure. Everything appeared just as I'd left it.

I needed to think, and I needed to think hard and fast. If Michelle hadn't called me, my ass woulda still been in the room when they picked up Honey. Maybe D had set me up, and she was tryin' to warn me. I had no idea who I could trust. Big seemed to be the only one not involved wit' anything, but at this point I was too shook to hit even him. Honey's Impala was hot. There was so much shit in it that they would have Honey locked up for a minimum of twenty-five. Would

she rat me out? Did they know 'bout Ro? I sat
down on the couch and stomped a spider as it
scurried from underneath it. Is this what God
felt like doin' when He looked down at me?

I was glad Honey didn't know the truth 'bout
me and Michelle. If I needed her to take the
wrap for a nigga there was no way she would do
it if she didn't think she was numba one. There
was nothin' in or on the car to tie it back to me. I
decided to go ahead and call Big Baby to see if he
could get through to anyone at the precinct who
would still cooperate wit' us.

"Yo, Rah, Monique from the telly jus' hit me—"

I cut him off before he could finish. "I need
you to hit T, an' any otha nigga you can safely
get to without raisin' any flags. We need to know
what they know." I didn't wait for Big to answer.
I didn't want to risk saying too much and com-
promising myself or him. I hung up and debated
on callin' Michelle. I didn't see any point. She
was pissed and I might as well take advantage of
her anger and use it as an excuse to lie low.

# While You Were Away

## 23

Rasheed didn't have to call for me to know what was going on. Every news station was covering the story about the drugs that were killing addicts, and the nineteen-year-old stripper calling herself a queen pen and taking the credit. The fact that she worked at the Hot Spot made it even more obvious to me why Rasheed had disappeared, but after a week of no contact I just couldn't figure out where the hell he'd disappeared to.

I tried calling and texting his cell but it was pointless; wherever he was he'd turned it off, probably for fear of having his calls traced via the cell phone towers. This entire situation solidified my point. It was time for Rah to get out of the drug game and the club business altogether. I'd been leaving Trey with Ris when I went to work because I was too paranoid that something would go down or get uncovered, and the first thing the police would do was snatch him out of his daycare. She was truly proving to be my life support and I was so thankful she put aside her anger at me leaving with Rah on vacation.

I spent more time in the familiar comfort of Ris's place than I did at my own house. I couldn't stand being alone in there, and often I had nightmares of men kicking in my front door with guns drawn, ready to drag me off to jail. It was just easier to completely lose myself in my work and try not to focus on the news, or the media. It was bad enough Heman-Shebitch knew Rah owned the Hot Spot. He'd already tried to put me on blast in front of my superiors the first day everything hit the news. We were in our morning meeting when he decided to put my business out there.

"So, Michelle, how on earth is your *baby daddy* dealing with all the press around his *club?*" He'd put extra emphasis on the words "baby daddy" and "club" as if to stress the fact that both were bad associations.

"Well, Mr. Soloman, my son's father is actually handling the event very well and is at this moment in Georgia opening a second establishment. I'm pretty sure he'll extend your VIP card to that one as well, just let him know when you're in town." I'd never in my life seen a black man blush, but Heman-Shebitch did just that and it was hilarious!

I smiled to myself at the memory as I pulled into Ris's driveway and gathered my things. She was nowhere to be found when I walked in and Trey was asleep atop a ton of pillows in the middle of the living room floor. His toys were everywhere and I couldn't resist kneeling down and kissing him on the cheek. He looked so much like Rah and yet so much like me. He was the best of both of us. I stood and made my way upstairs to find Ris. She'd decided to use Trey's nap as a break to hop in the shower, and I decided to let her have her peace and went back downstairs, determined to cook something for dinner. I'd decided I had a taste for meatloaf and mashed potatoes, and prayed what I needed was in the fridge because I sure as hell didn't feel like going back out to the grocery store.

"Damn, momma, when the hell did you get here?" Ris burst into the kitchen in a fresh, familiar breeze of mango butter. She'd obviously been in my shower bag again.

"Well hello to you too, and how was your day?" I swore I needed to school her ass on how to properly greet someone. She'd taken a seat at the kitchen counter across from me and sat quietly. That was definitely not like Ris. I squinted slightly as I examined her sitting across from me, trying to figure out why she was suddenly so demure. She was avoiding my eyes; her gaze moved lazily around the kitchen, focusing on everything and nothing.

"Bitch, are you high?" I didn't need an answer. Her shower this late in the day, red eyes, and full-moon pupils said it all. I couldn't believe she had the audacity to get high while Trey was in the house with her.

"Before you fly off the handle, Chelle, I'm . . . I mean we are goin' through a lot right now and my ass is on the verge of a meltdown. I was thinkin' of all the worst shit that could go wrong and I just got overwhelmed. I was wound too tight and needed to unwind."

I was not used to "high" Ris; all my experiences centered around "drunk" Ris. She wasn't cursing, she wasn't buzzing around me in a frenzy of adult ADHD-directed energy. She just calmly sat in front of me as if we were discussing the news. In a sense it was wrong of me to force my situation on her.

"I'm sorry, Risi cup. But, damn, you could have at least waited until I got here. I would have understood."

"Girl, Trey was 'sleep long before I did that shit. I fixed him a mini margarita and it musta knocked his li'l ass out cold."

The knife I was using to cut up the potatoes stilled in my hand and I glared. *If this heffa . . .*

"Damn. Chelle, where is yo' sense of humor? I ain't give the baby a drink. We went and ran all over the park this morning and I fixed him a big lunch. He's fine. Li'l nigga just got the itis extra hard." She laughed lazily and slapped her leg almost in slow motion.

I definitely was not used to "high" Ris, because that shit was definitely not funny.

"Nah, but seriously, Chelle. You know I've got a lot on my mind. I sit and watch the news all day and I can't help but worry." She looked like she was about to cry and I started to feel even worse for, once again, dragging Larissa into my and Rasheed's mess. I walked over and hugged her, focused on getting her out of the pessimistic funk she'd managed to slip into.

"I'ma need ya ass to read a book or something during the day, ma. Everything is going to be fine as long as you keep thinking it is going to be fine. The second we start talkin' negative we give that negative energy power."

Trey woke up and stumbled his way into the kitchen, looking too much like a drunken little man for us both not to find it hilarious.

"You sure you ain't give my baby a drink?" I asked as I scooped him up and pulled his Binky out of his mouth to plant a kiss on his smiling little face. Daddy or no daddy, he was going to be all right. We were both going to be all right.

After dinner I slipped outside to make a quick phone call without stressin' Ris out. I needed more details on what was going on and I was curious as to how well everything was going over with the DEA. I called the only person who I knew would give me solid information.

"Hey, darlin', how are you holdin' up?" It was good to hear Derrick's warm, comforting voice over the phone.

"I'm okay, sweetheart. Can we meet this evening? I have a few things I'd like to go over with you." I didn't want to say anything specific over the phone. For all I knew, Derrick could be under surveillance.

"No problem, Chelle. Our usual?"

"You know it."

# Honeycomb Hideout

## 24

Almost a month had passed since Honey had been picked up and I still hadn't heard from her. T was the only nigga not scared of the new chief and pretty much kept us filled in on what was goin' on. Turned out Honey wasn't talkin', well, at least not 'bout me anyway. She told the DEA the drugs in the car were hers and that she was runnin' the entire operation. She even owned up to puttin' Inferno on the streets and claimed she was drivin' in fresh supply since there were complications with the batches out now. And those muthafuckas were actually believin' her.

I'd lost 'round ten pounds, and hadn't seen anyone. I did buy a prepaid cell at a 7-Eleven 'round the corner, but no one had the number 'cept Big Baby. He was steady keepin' tabs on Derrick and lettin' me know the nigga's moves. He'd been meeting Michelle at restaurants and some otha bullshit, but I always cut Big off. I couldn't stand to hear the details knowin' I couldn't leave to hand that nigga his ass.

Michelle was pro'ly worried to death by now and probably usin' D as an outlet since I'd left her high and dry, but I still couldn't take any chances. My reign in the drug world was at its peak and I wasn't tryin' to be greeted by jail bars on the downslope. DEA, FBI, CIA; shit, I bet not a single one of them alphabet bitches would sleep if they had any idea Honey was a key to unlockin' my empire.

I'd only left my safe house twice: once to buy the cell, and again to stock up on groceries and basic shit. The alarm on my phone went off. I'd set a reminder. Today was Honey's first day in court. I didn't know if they really believed her, or if it was all an act to bring me out into the open but, secretly, I prayed they believed her. All operations had ceased and our only revenue comin' in was from the club. Big said they did a small investigation since they knew Honey worked there, but the club checked out clean. I'd always made sure of that.

I called Big Baby. "Any news?"

He sounded as tired as I felt. "Nah, you know I'ma drop word soon as we know what she get. Rumors say her crackhead cousin blackmailed her and then dropped dime when Honey couldn't get her any product. She dug her own grave by ownin' up to erethang though. Me and the boys been playin' in the dirt, but you know we got our eyes an' ears open."

Playin' in the dirt meant everybody was bein' smart. Lyin' low. I didn't have anything else to say. The waiting game had begun and I couldn't do anything but wait.

"All right, hit me soon as you hear somethin'. Be easy."

It felt like forever. It took them two months of court cases and plea bargainin' before I finally got the call. Honey got the maximum: life in prison with a mandatory minimum of twenty-five years. I had so much ridin' on the verdict, and when it finally hit I felt sadness, joy, triumph, and even disgust. T hit Big and said with Honey locked up and sales droppin', his chief closed the books on Inferno. I needed to talk to Honey, tell her how sorry and how grateful I was for her. I was torn between celebratin' and mournin'.

I'd asked T to set up a phone call with Honey as soon as he could. My cell rang with a number I didn't recognize. With the case closed, I wasn't as apprehensive about pickin' up.

"You have a collect call from . . ."

"Trenisha Davis."

"Do you accept?"

My throat instantly went dry as if I were chokin' on a piece of dry, stale bread with no water anywhere in sight. I hadn't heard her voice in so long, I'd forgotten how she sounded.

"I accept."

"Hey, daddy. How's life?" She didn't even sound like herself.

"Not so good, sunshine, how are you?" I couldn't believe our conversation. Here I was free, speakin' to a woman who gave up erethin' for my freedom. A tear burned a hot trail down my cheek, splashin' onto my jeans, markin' the small spot dark blue. I focused on that spot and mentally manned up as I waited for Honey to answer my question.

"We are good, baby. I never got a chance to tell you thank you. I wasn't eva gonna be more than a strippa, workin' day by day to get by. You helped me see and do thangs no one eva bothered to do for me. You got so much ambition, daddy, so much drive. Without you, I woulda killed myself. I owe my life to you. I owe our lives to you. I'm pregnant, Rasheed."

My mouth fell open in shock. Those were not the words I was expectin' to hear. Honey was havin' my baby—in prison?

"Fuck, baby. I'm so sorry, I . . ." What do you say to someone who's given up so much when you selfishly gave up so little? For one of the few times in my life I was at a loss for words.

"It's okay, Rah, she's gonna be here in February. Jus' promise me you'll take care of her for me, daddy."

"Damn, girl, we actually havin' a li'l girl?" I couldn't even see me with a daughter. I ran one of the most successful strip clubs on the East Coast. I done hit and quit more women in the last year than some niggas seen in a lifetime. And I was gonna be raisin' a li'l girl.

"Yes, daddy. I ain't want to tell you this way. I pictured it so much different than this shit right here. But now you know I love yo' ass for real. You my heart, Rasheed."

I lowered my head and sighed. I couldn't hold back anymore and the tears fell freely, trailin' rivers of sorrow down my cheeks. I had to check myself quick before I fucked up and said something incriminating.

"I know you love me, girl. You ain't have to prove a damn thang to no-damn-body. You keep my baby fed. Guess my ass gonna have to get used to buyin' a bunch of pink shit, huh?" Honey laughed her same old laugh that made me remember summer days ridin' in the car, sneakin' off to fuck in the club, and too much shit I took for granted.

I made Honey promise to call me again as soon as possible. I felt like a freed man as I stepped outside my self-made prison into the calm, cool October air. A young couple strolled past me, heads bent close together as they talked and held hands. The leaves had turned all different shades of bright yellow, orange, and red, clearly indicatin' cuffin' season had begun. That time of year when you find someone to cozy up to for some warm company through the winter. Guess it was as perfect a time as any for me to cozy back up to Michelle. A weight had been lifted from my shoulders only to be replaced by a looming cloud of hurt and contempt caused by missing Honey.

I hadn't seen or spoken to Michelle in nearly three months. I missed my son. Months of livin' in the shadows made me miss life all together. I turned on my old cell I'd kept charged up on the floor just for this day, and called Michelle's phone.

"Rah?" Worry, excitement, love; it's amazing how I heard so much in the way she said my name.

"Yes, baby. It's me. I'm on my way home."

# John 3:16

# 25

The house was just as I'd left it. Shit. It looked like Michelle hadn't even lived there for the full three months I was gone. There was definitely an unspoken tension between us. She wanted to know what happened and who this stripper was who was takin' the blame for all of my hard work, and I didn't want to talk about it. The first few days were awkward but, as time went on, we gradually got back into our rhythm.

It was December and I'd only spoken to Honey twice since our initial conversation, once to get all her into to make sure her card had money on it for her to eat right with the baby. She was five months along and the baby was kickin' her ass. From the little convo we had she was havin' a hard time keepin' food down and they were monitoring her to make sure the baby was growin' okay. I remembered Michelle had that same problem and would sip peppermint tea to calm her stomach. I made a mental note to send her some in a care package.

The second time we spoke we actually got in a damn argument. She was goin' on 'bout some chick she was cellmates with. Sounded like some straight-up dike shit to me. I mean, how many niggas want to hear they girl goin' on and on 'bout anotha bitch takin' care of 'em. Washin' clothes, braidin' her hair, so I asked Honey if the bitch was eatin' her pussy, too. She started to tell me somethin' 'bout the girl but I'd hung up on her ass. I'd make sure Honey was comfortable. I owed her a great deal for what she was doin'. But I wasn't gonna be happy 'bout her dikin' or no dumb shit like that.

It was one of those typical December days where it felt like you were frozen the second you stepped outdoors and not a ray of sun could be seen through the thick white winter clouds. We were two weeks from Christmas, and I felt like my life was finally startin' to get back to normal. Me and Chelle were out pickin' up toys for Trey when my cell went off. It was Big and he didn't sound good. I promised to meet him at the club soon as me and Michelle was done. I dropped Chelle off at the house and drove the quick ten minutes to the club. *Shit betta be important*. We were gonna put the tree up tonight and Trey was so excited he'd been askin' nonstop for the last week.

I pulled up and parked beside Big's Durango. The usually polished-up jet-black truck looked pathetic. Dried mud splatters covered it from tire to mid-door. I meant to joke the nigga thoroughly.

"Nigga, you been out muddin' wit' dem white boys or som'n?" Big Baby was sittin' at the bar wit' Chris, and anotha nigga I'd seen around but didn't know.

"Rah, whatup." Big got up to greet me as the other two sat like gargoyle statues, heads down and quiet.

"Rememba that shit you asked me to take care of befo' shit got hot? That situation."

I nodded.

"Well, these the two niggas who worked off that fifty grand you gave me."

"It's done?" I couldn't believe my ears.

"Yeah, nig. Wasn't much to it. My soldiers thorough like that."

"Well shit, sound like we need to have us a fuckin' celebration. All dances, drinks, whateva the fuck y'all want on me tonight, niggas. Y'all VIP in this bitch!"

Neither of the two niggas budged. I was frontin' extra hard, puttin' on airs like I was God Almighty and my lightning bolt hit its mark. We shoulda all been throwin' back shots by now, commendin' each other for mowin' over the snake in our grass instead of steppin' around it. Instead, I was greeted by silence and long faces that mirrored the shame and disgust I myself felt pulling at the pit of my stomach. My confidant, homeboy, hell the nigga I called brother was no more. I'd slain Able and underneath all my bravado I still felt a sinner's shame. I took a seat beside Chris at the bar. He looked like he was on the verge of bein' sick.

"Well, nigga, guess I got ya cherry the way you lookin' right now. We all been there. You good, right?" He didn't even look at me. We both jumped as a chair clamored to the floor. His boy stood abruptly and walked outside.

"Nah, Rah, my hands been bloody, nigga. When shit got hot Big told us hold off on the contract. I ain't a patient nigga but I waited. I was so fuckin' amped. I really needed dat dough. A few weeks ago, Big said it was on again, so I camped out an' hit the nigga at night when he was pullin' up at his crib. I swear, I ain' know, man. I pulled up beside the car but . . ." Chris's voice broke and he lowered his head into his hands.

Frustrated, eyebrow raised, I looked up at Big for clarification. If this nigga was 'bout to have a breakdown and run off to confess some shit, I might have to have him taken care of.

Big Baby cleared his throat hard and looked away. His usually boisterous voice was barely above a whisper. "Rah . . . they got the kid too."

My heart sank in my chest. The phrase "casualty of war" floated 'round in my head.

"Chris, I need to know what happened." All I could think 'bout was how the fuck I dodged one bullet to get hit by anotha. If Danita found out, it was gonna be the end fa sure. Chris gave me a recap. They pulled up beside Derrick as he'd jus' got home from the grocery store. Chris's boy was drivin' and Chris was the one who opened fire. He didn't see the li'l boy asleep in the back seat 'til it was too late. I said a silent prayer for forgiveness. At least the li'l nigga died in his sleep.

Nothin' was goin' right. I was startin' to feel defeated. I needed to figure out how the fuck I was gonna get through this. I wondered if Michelle knew what had happened yet. I left the club, pullin' my keys out of my pocket, and walked out into a cold, grey, misting rain. The weather matched my mood perfectly. I couldn't believe I was responsible for the death of Danita's son. His face was hauntin' me, eyes like Dee's, lips like Dee's.

What the fuck had I done? Derrick may have deserved what he had comin', but not the kid. Hell, I didn't even know the li'l nigga's name. I sat in my car for a few minutes, tryin' to figure out how I would face my own son, or even Michelle for that matter. Shit, I ain' pull the trigga, but I ain't warn them niggas eitha.

Michelle called my cell and I simply hit the ignore button. I couldn't talk to her right then. I jus' needed to put this shit behind me an' man up. This was the life I chose. Mufuckas come an' go. Derrick chose to disrespect me in the biz an' on the personal. He was a liability I couldn't afford. I put the car in drive and drove home, content that what was done needed to be done. I would deal wit' Danita when the issue arose. No one knew her son was with Derrick, and Big said they'd driven the bodies out into the woods and buried 'em afterward. Hopefully, it would be a while before she got any idea what had happened.

I parked outside my house. The blinds were open and I could see Chelle and Trey sittin' in front of the TV. I gave myself the luxury of imaginin' it was Honey wit' a li'l girl who looked jus' like her. I shook my head to clear the image of my caged angel. She was on the verge of suicide before me, before I gave her a job at the club.

Maybe her role in my life was exactly how she played it. I walked into my home and hugged Michelle and Trey. Maybe it was time I worked on bein' a new, betta nigga for her. Too many people were bein' bodied behind the old me.

The holiday wasn't goin' by as easily as I thought it would. As much as I appreciated Chelle and Trey, I felt like shit ere time I thought 'bout Honey and my baby girl in prison. I was gradually sinkin' into a depression, and not havin' my ace there to talk shit out was leavin' me no choice but to hold erething in. I didn't sleep much. My guilty conscience kept me awake most nights, and when I did try to sleep I had nightmares. Even though Michelle could sense somethin' was wrong, she never said anything. I was startin' to think she knew 'bout Derrick and maybe felt jus' as guilty as I was feelin'.

I'd been spendin' more and more time at the club. I didn't want anyone pushin' product for a while. We needed to wait 'til I was sure shit had cooled off. The brothas weren't happy, but they undastood and did whateva they needed to do so their fams could have a good Christmas. I was in my office when Diamond came in.

"Merry Christmas, Rah. I know you ain't gonna spend Christmas Eve waitin' for Santa wit' us."

I wasn't sure why I'd decided to keep the place open, but som'n told me there might be a few lonely-ass niggas or angry baby daddies who ain't wanna be alone. I was right; it almost looked like any otha night.

"Whatup, Di? You come in here to give me my present or what?" It'd been a while since I'd done anything. I guessed stress'd do that to a nigga.

Diamond was standin' there in her festive-ass Mrs. Claus outfit. She had on a stripper's version of one anyway: red fishnets and knee-high black leather boots. Her weave was so long it hung down to her ass, and she was lickin' her full lips, waitin' for me to finish my eye exam. I sat on top of my desk and extended my finger for her to come over. It went without sayin'; she knew what was up and kneeled in between my legs. She undid my pants and slid my dick out through the slit in my boxers. I was immediately straight as an arrow as I closed my eyes. Damn it'd been a minute. I jus' knew I was gonna embarrass myself and bust right there in her hand.

I looked down an' watched Diamond wrap her lips 'round my dick. I put my head back and tried to enjoy the moment, but my mind was still distracted. I needed to get home and put Trey's

Power Wheel Escalade together. I'd bought Chelle an engagement ring and was gonna propose to her in the mornin'. I figured proposin' meant I'd have at least anotha year or two before we'd have to walk down the aisle. I was gonna do my best to make her happy. Guessed I would start that shit tomorrow. Diamond was goin' in and a nigga was 'bout to let the fuck go. I wrapped my fingers in her weave and forced myself farther down her throat.

My heart was slammin' in my ears and the music from the club drowned out Diamond's moans as she sucked every fuckin' drop outta me. I heard my office door close and jumped, snappin' my eyes in its direction. *Musta been Big Baby*. I smiled down at Diamond.

"Damn Di! You know you jus' earned the night off, right?"

"Boy, stop! I ain't got no fuckin' kids. I'm 'bout to go out he' an' get this mufuckin' papa. Them niggas is depressed an' droppin' dolla's!"

I chuckled. Diamond was always 'bout gettin' her money, that was for sure.

"All right, momma. Go handle ya biz." I smacked her on the ass as she hopped up and sashayed outta my office.

Well, now that I'd gotten that outta my system. *Whew*. Ya boy was feelin' ready to take on the

world. I buttoned my pants, makin' sure I looked
presentable before headin' out to find Big Baby. He
was standin' ova by the bar, talkin' to Annette.

"Yo, was you lookin' fa me?" He shook his
head no and leaned toward me so I could hear
him ova the music.

"Yo, ya girl can cook her ass off. Rah, you one
lucky nigga."

"What girl? What the hell you talkin' 'bout?"
*Damn. Big Shirley musta brought plates.* My
eyes roved the crowd, lookin' for her so I could
ask for mine.

"Damn, nigga. Don't tell me you in da dog-
house again. Chelle must *really* be pissed if she
came out the house to bring erebody a dinner
plate 'cept yo' ass!"

A lump had formed in my throat. All the en-
thusiasm and relief I felt a few moments ago
evaporated instantly. No, I didn't see Michelle.
But I was sure as fuck she'd seen me.

# Heart for a Heart

## 26

I walked back to my office and sat at my desk. I knew Michelle well enough to know she'd run home, grab Trey, and go either to her mom's or one of her girls' cribs. I knew she'd seen Diamond toppin' me off, and for once I had no explanation. Here I was ready to propose to her, tryin' to do right by her, hell, I was even thinkin' 'bout her while I was gettin' head. And I was still fuckin' up.

I spent Christmas Day alone. The tree was eerie and dark with all of Trey's presents wrapped and piled up underneath it. I flipped on the TV more for background noise than anything. The remote fell from my hand, crashin' onto the floor after bashin' my foot. Shock and pain seared through my core like lightning. A special report bulletin streamed across the screen, putting me face to face with my demons.

Derrick never smiled in any of his pictures and the irony was foreboding, as his sarcastic smirk now mocked my manhood, reminding me of the blood on my hands. Stains on my soul. The hair on the back of my neck was on edge, and I felt ice cold inside and out as I stared at the image of my eighteen-year-old partner in crime. Lack of a recent photo made the news crew resort to using D's high school photo. I always considered myself a calculated, heartless, cold-blooded nigga. You could walk up to ten muthafuckas on the street and any of 'em would say Rasheed was a boss-ass dude. Name anyone who ever did me wrong and I could tell you off top that they ass was met with an appropriate consequence.

Suddenly, none of that bullshit meant anything to me as the news reporter mentioned the li'l boy slain along with Derrick. Tears clouded my vision as everything that reminded me of Danita burned into the upper left corner of my flat screen. A frail, dark-skinned elderly woman was kneeling with a football clutched to her chest, head lowered with a pain so evident the news reporter stood by, outwardly emotional and at a loss for words. The old woman was Danita's great aunt and only surviving relative.

I'd always considered myself a goon, a thug, a warrior. But nothing in or out of this world could

have possibly prepared me for the moment my
heart shattered into stone shards and stabbed
me back a thousand times harder than any blade
or screwdriver ever had. The news reporter de-
scribed the area in Hampton where D lived as
a "war zone." Kids had gathered on a street corner and were laying toy trucks and teddy bears
down at a cross that displayed the boy's photo.
His name seared itself into my cornea; etched
forever into my memory, just the same as it was
engraved in jagged script into the roughly made
white wooden cross and plastered on my screen
in stark white letters: *Rasheed Lavan White Jr.*

A man had found the bodies while out hikin'
in the woods lookin' for a Christmas tree. Just
my luck he'd pick the tree next to the shallow
grave Big Baby and his boys dug. The ground
must have been next to impossible to get a
shovel into with it bein' so cold. They did a piss-
ass job. The media had been kept out of the loop
until they could properly ID the bodies and no-
tify the families.

My legs crumpled from beneath me and I sank
to the floor in a lump of misery and contempt.
I hated my life, I hated what I'd become, and I
could never take back what the fuck I'd done.
I tried to replay every second of my encounter
with the curly haired li'l boy who was my exact

complexion with Danita's looks. He was too tall for his age, pro'ly because I was the same way when I was that age. I didn't even know she was pregnant. Why the fuck didn't she tell me? She musta jus' found out, couldn't have been no more than a month along when I'd caught her stealin' from me. The physical pain that contorted my body and gripped my insides was nothing I'd ever felt before. I cried for my oldest son who I was supposed to be takin' care of, and I cried for the pain of not havin' the chance to get to know the li'l nigga who was my junior. The realization that I *was* a senior weighed on my chest like a herd of elephants. Anger seared through me aimed solely at Danita; she should have fuckin' told me! I wouldn't have believed her, but she could have at least *tried* to tell me!

I don't know how long I lay on the floor, but it had started to get dark outside. My cell rang. I didn't recognize the number, but I was certain it was Honey. For the first time since she'd been locked up I had absolutely nothing to say to her and I ignored the call. I stayed in that same spot until I fell asleep. I felt cold, miserable, drained, and all I wanted to do was stay asleep. My phone went off and pulled me back to reality. It was a text from Big Baby.

Accordin' to the news they were launchin' an investigation to determine who committed the murders and the motive behind it. He needed me to meet him at the club in twenty. Self-preservation kicked in and I forced myself up to shower. *I might have to take care of Chris and his boy.* How much more money would it cost me to bury this forever?

I pulled up beside Big Baby's Durango and gathered my thoughts. I had roughly one mil in the safe, I figured $200K would be enough to keep us outta trouble. I got out of my car and started to make my way into the club. I heard everything before I saw it. Black undercover police cars zoomed in at me from all directions, completely surroundin' me. They swarmed and buzzed around me as a dozen barrels now bull's-eyed my forehead. I gave T a puzzled glance as he got outta one of the cars and walked over to me, weapon drawn.

"Nigga! What the fuck is goin' on? You need to call ya dogs off!" I tried to keep my voice as calm as possible, fear makin' my hands shake and sweat.

"I'm sorry, Rasheed. It's over, man. Get down on the ground."

"What the fuck for? I ain't did a muthafuckin' thing, nigga! All the money I done laced y'all bitches wit' and I can't even get approached with respect?" I was livid. I stood beside my car and stared into a sea of familiar faces. I'd paid these niggas, clothed they kids when they li'l bullshit-ass police salary wasn't cuttin' it, entertained they dumb asses on my own fuckin' dollar, and they had the fuckin' nerve to come at me like this? I had a pistol under the driver's seat in my car. I could just say fuck it and go out in a blaze of glory like Denzel in *Training Day*. Take a few of these bitches with me.

"Y'all can at least tell me what the fuck you tryin' to arrest me for!" A pudgy white cocksucker got the balls to raise his voice up. He was obviously the new chief.

"Rasheed Lavan White Sr., you are under arrest for the murders of Derrick Richards an' Rasheed Lavan White Jr."

His voice hit me like a death sentence. My stomach twisted and I just knew I was gonna be sick. I felt like a trapped pit bull. I was trained to fight and kill. Fight poverty, fight the system, fight other niggas. If I wanted to solidify my place at the top I had to fight and kill or be killed. I faced the same corrupt muthafuckas who helped me become the monster I was, and I fought every instinct that drove me to fight and kill even now, with all the odds stacked against me. My eyes roved around, lookin' for an escape, some way out. Big Baby was sittin' in the back of one of the other cars and a few cops were walkin' out of the club with some of my stuff in plastic bags. My time was up. I turned my back and raised my hands over my head and felt the wind get knocked out of me as I was tackled to the hard, dank ground. I was searched and hefted up to my feet, my hands were cuffed in front of me, and I was placed in the back of T's car.

He got in and handed me an envelope through the chicken wire separator.

"My nigga, I couldn't give y'all any kinda heads-up. Shit hit me jus' as I reported for my shift. I been out on vacation for Christmas. When the word got to me that they were tellin' Danita who killed her son, I ain't have no time to warn anyone." He was lookin' straight ahead as he drove me to the precinct, mouth barely movin' as he spoke.

"You were an honestly loyal nigga, Rah. I'm so sorry, dawg. You know I always appreciated you, nigga. But, God, I'm sorry. She ain't deserve that shit."

"T, what the fuck you talkin' 'bout, nigga?"

We pulled up at a light and he turned slightly so he could see me outta the corner of his eye. "'Bout Honey. I'm so sorry, nigga." He cleared his throat.

"Honey was cellmates wit' Danita. They seemed to been gettin' along fine. Honey was waitin' on a spot in the maternity ward an' was s'posed to get moved today."

I was still lost. Honey was in prison wit' Dee? That's who she was dikin' wit'?

"They found Honey this mornin'. I guess when Danita got news 'bout her son she went off. She stabbed Honey, Rasheed. An' then she used the shank an' killed herself. You got a li'l girl, nigga. She was born this mornin'." He took a deep breath. "Honey lost too much blood; she's not gonna make it. My boy works ova at the prison an' found that letter when they went to clear the cell. He knew I'd get it to you."

I looked down at the letter, and the paper darkened in a spot as a tear slid down my cheek.

"You need to read it quick, I don't know if anything's in it that might hurt ya case, but they ain't gonna let you keep it when we get to processing."

All I could do was nod at T, and I opened the letter.

*Hey daddy,*

We ain't really been talkin lately so Dee suggested I write you sometimes. I miss you so much baby. The girls in here are ok. Now they know I'm pregnant so it's not too many bitches that'll fuck wit me. I was mad as hell at u for hangin' up on me cuz Dee ain't no dike baby. She actually used to be one of ya girlfriends a long time ago. She told me bout y'all and I ain't even get mad cuz that was waaay before you knew me. Baby, Dee told me what happened an that you had her face cut up. She refuse to tell you herself but she was pregnant wit y'all's son and was tryin to get money for an abortion, she wasn't stealin from u. Your baby mama called her an' told her bout y'all an' you broke her heart, baby. She say you takin care of him now so I'm hopin you bondin' wit your son. If you ain figured it out for yourself yet, then yes that's what I'm telling u. I seen his picture an he look like a mini U! He so cute. I wish I could be there, I'ma need u to be a good man and not let him pick on Paris when she come. I hope you ok wit da name. I always wanted to go and I'm hopin she will get to one day. Thank you for the extra money on my card for Christmas.

*Paris got me up in here eatin' honey buns, Fritos, anything I can get my hands on. I love you, daddy. I'ma try to call you on Christmas Day, but if not then I'ma put this in the mail to the club.*

*xoxoxo Honey—ps in case you didn't know them lil xo's I wrote mean hugs an kisses.*

# Baby Momma

## 27

I parked across the street and watched as Rasheed was handcuffed and placed into a police car. My windshield was the movie screen and I was sitting front and center in the director's chair. I'd spent the last eight years directin' my ass off and this was the grand finale. Some women professionally chase athletes, actors, and rappers. They look for anyone who can turn their broke and ordinary lives into a fairy tale. You'll see 'em running behind these niggas with Cinderella dreams, hoping and praying that if they suck and fuck him just right, maybe they'll get spoiled and catered to. Hoping if they put it down better than all the other women on his roster, they'll eventually win the grand prize and be the Mrs. Married to the money and the misery, constantly fighting off younger, better-looking competition.

Then you have women like me. We stuck with the nobodies through whatever we had to, and helped turn them into that successful rapper or basketball player, praying they didn't leave us for another woman after all was said and done. Well, that's my story with Rasheed, anyway. From the beginning he'd always been determined to be a "have," makin' profit off of the "have-nots."

We first met at a party he was having at his aunt's house when I was sixteen. Back then his vision was no bigger than making enough to buy the next pair of Jordans, but I saw more. Rasheed could have been good at anything he put his mind to. Not only did he have the drive and intelligence, but he looked damn good, still does. We, being from two different worlds had people shocked when we first started dating. It took me a little getting used to as well, but let me just say it wasn't hard to adjust to a six foot plus well-built nigga with all the right tools in his toolbox.

It was always my personal goal to turn Rah into the successful man I knew he could be. He knew the streets and he knew the drug game. I went to college for business but you might as well say we both got a degree out of the deal. I brought home everything I learned about investing and marketing, and I molded a nickel-and-dime corner boy into a business-savvy boss nigga.

I always knew there would be a day when I would need to make up my mind: choose the life I wanted over the life I was living, or sit back and accept things and just remain miserable. When things with Rasheed were good and he was consciously trying to do right by me, life was great. But our bad memories far outweighed the good ones. I'd fallen out of love with Rasheed a long time ago. In the beginning, I loved him so much that I sometimes blamed myself for him cheating on me, lying to me, treating me like I was nothing. I became one of those women I despised. I wanted the money and the fairy tale. I wanted the companionship, huge wedding, possibly three kids, and beautiful home.

My BlackBerry buzzed from somewhere in the bottom of my purse. Digging to find it, I wondered why I didn't just put the damn thing in my pants pocket. I finally located it and smiled at Larissa's picture smiling back at me on the caller ID.

"Hey, sweetie, I was just thinkin' about you."

"I bet you were! I be thinkin' 'bout me a damn lot too."

I laughed. Ris was probably the only person I knew who could fit "damn" or "fuck" in between any regular phrase to make a new one, and she was cocky with it too.

"Is everything okay? Trey's not actin' up, is he?" I asked.

"You know he's fine but, Chelly, really, are you okay right now?"

She sounded so concerned, and I honestly didn't think I'd given reality a chance to really sink in. Maybe because I'd already imagined this day a thousand times in my head. Or, maybe, because in my spirit I felt like this was the way things needed to be and I accepted it as such. I took a deep breath. I needed to wrap my mind around what I'd done—what we'd done.

"Yes, Ris, I'm really okay, I promise." I tried to add a little lightness to my tone to put her at ease.

"Good, 'cause we been puttin' up wit' dat nigga's bullshit long e-fuckin'-nough. He too stupid to 'preciate a good bitch when he got one, then fuck 'em!"

Me and Ris had had this conversation so many times. Me going through drama, trying to leave Rah only to turn around and give him chance after chance. Except this time the conversation was entirely different, this time her words were reality.

"I know, girl, I know. He just got picked up. I need to go home, grab a few things, and then I'll be over," I told her.

"Well hurry up, 'cause I got us a couple bottles an' we pop-pop-poppin' dem bitches tonight!"

I pulled up at what Ris liked to call her mini mansion, the place I always referred to it as my getaway. My house with Rasheed was home only when it was convenient for him. I had just left from over there and I stayed just long enough to grab a few of Trey's toys and his favorite pj's. The lights were out on the tree and the place looked exactly how I finally felt inside about Rasheed: empty. I had absolutely nothing left for him.

I saw Ris appear in the front door, holding Trey, before I could even put the car in park.

"Look, Trey, there's Mommeeee! Say Merry Christmas, Mommy!"

I couldn't help but smile. He did his best, but could only get out what sounded like "Ma-Chris, Mommy." He was the only good thing Rasheed had ever given me.

"Aw, hello, my babies." I kissed them both on the cheek. "Let's get inside. It's cold, feels like it might snow." I followed them inside, glad to be out of the cold.

Ris's mini mansion was exactly that; there were five bedrooms, two and a half baths, it even had fireplaces in the master bedroom and family room. Everything was decorated in warm, comfy colors: dark chocolate and green, tan, and blues.

It had a real modern, cozy feel to it. My touch consisted of a few bright yellow throw pillows that were lyin' on the floor, indicating Trey had been playing around. Ris liked to burn patchouli candles in just about every room, and the scent always reminded me of her and subconsciously I relaxed. I sat in front of the fireplace in the living room, enjoying the painful tingle as my fingers and toes warmed up while Ris went to put Trey down for the night. The police would probably be contacting me for a statement or something to that degree. I seriously needed to pull myself together.

"I wasn't sure if you would be hungry or not. I ordered pizza for me an' Trey if you want some."

Lost in my thoughts, I didn't even hear Larissa come back downstairs. "Thank you, sweetie. I'm good right now. I could really use a glass of that champagne, though."

"Girl, you ain't said nothin' but a mufuckin' word! I got Patrón an' . . ." The rest of her sentence trailed off as she scampered into the kitchen.

I shook my head. Messing around with this girl would have my face in the toilet all day tomorrow if she had her way. She used to get me so messed up when we were in college. Ris could probably drink most niggas under the table if she put her mind to it.

"Whoo! Baby, we toastin' tonight!" Ris returned, dancing toward me, and landed on the couch, clanking champagne glasses between her fingers.

"Yeah, I guess we can start our celebration a little early. Shit ain't over until the gavel drops but we can talk about that some other time. Pour my ass a draank."

Ris fought with the cork for a few seconds before it went flying out of the bottle with a loud "pop." We toasted to ourselves. I'd never been a huge fan of champagne, especially the dry stuff; tastes like grapefruit rinds and club soda, if you asked me. But Ris loved it, and if she was buying you had no choice but drink what she liked to drink.

I hadn't eaten much today so it wouldn't take more than a couple of glasses to get me completely fucked up. I needed to pace myself. I sure as hell ain't want a headache to fight with in the morning. We sat in silence, enjoying the relaxing warmth from the fire. The orange glow danced off of the walls, reminding me of a summer sunset—reminding me of my last night in the Bahamas with Rah. That was my last good memory of us together. Giggling and teasing each other, kissing like we were back in high school and nothing could ever come between us. Ris set her glass on the coffee table in front of the couch and turned to face me, her demeanor suddenly serious and quiet.

"Michelle, how long have we known each other?" she asked.

"Shit, girl, I don't know. Feels like *forever!* Why, what the hell you done went and did now?" Usually when Ris got quiet on me it was time for a confession, like the time she used my credit card to order a five-hundred-dollar wig off the Internet, or when she got our initials tattooed on the back of her neck. Ris never did anything small or half-assed. I had to give her credit for having balls when it came to living life.

"Baby, marry me."

I stared at her wide-eyed with disbelief. I was waiting for a giggle or a laugh, something to signal this was a joke. When none came, I realized Ris was actually being dead serious. I couldn't believe my ears. We'd been together so long and we'd been dealing with the issue of me and Rasheed for so many years that I never considered the possibility of marriage. What would my parents think? Hell, what would my friends and neighbors think?

"Ris, baby, I . . . I don't know what to say right now." My eyes filled with tears. It was just too much coming at me too soon, and too fast. I wasn't even fully at grips with what we'd done to Rasheed and, now, another life-changing decision. I did my best to keep my voice from shaking as I looked into Ris's hurt-filled emerald eyes that were slowly brimming with tears.

"You know I'm not like you with this whole thing. Ris, I'm not out. My job is so conservative. Baby, I'm almost a VP and it's taken me so long to get to this point." I didn't know what else to say. Yes, I loved Larissa, but for some reason I always kept a picture in the back of my mind of myself finally married to a man, married to Rasheed. It was selfish of me to go between the two of them like I'd been doing, and without Rah in the picture I really needed Ris to be there for me.

When I met Ris in college, I was still dating Rah. Some skank named Katrice had gone through Rah's cell and called me, asking who I was and why I was calling her man. That was the same night he claimed he was in a fight with some guys trying to cut in on his territory, and they got in a fight, putting him in the hospital with a knife wound to his shoulder. I was pretty sure ol' girl did it, but it was also the first time I'd ever dealt with Rah cheating on me and lying to me, and I took it hard. He always acted so in love and so faithful. Saying the right things, doing the right things, I couldn't imagine him kissing, loving, or even fuckin' another woman. Yeah, I had ulterior motives going in but he didn't know any of that, and I couldn't help fallin' in love with him.

Back then, I was too into Rah to even notice Ris was infatuated with me. It was my first year in college and I was still trying to adjust to the whole dorm lifestyle. I remembered meeting my new roommate, who was this beautiful honey-skinned woman with eyes the color of one of those jade dragons you see in Chinese restaurants. I always envied her long, thick reddish brown hair and killer body. I initially couldn't figure out why she was never with any guys, or why she never had any boyfriends. Even then I should have known Rah was a dawg. Ris told me he'd tried to holla at her one day when he came to see me on campus and I wasn't in my room. I defended him, told her she was probably just misreading his signals. Of course, when I confronted him about it he agreed with me, calling Ris a hater, and said she was probably just jealous that I had a man and she didn't.

The first time Rasheed broke my heart, it was Larissa who mended it back together. I'd always looked at other women's bodies and tried to imagine if I were a man what would be attractive to me. What kind of woman would I want to have in my arms? Would she be light-skinned, did pretty feet really matter, would I take personality over a fat ass? I'd always hated my height; my size often made me feel like less of a woman when I towered over smaller chicks. I found myself admiring Ris. She might have only been five one or so, but what she lacked in height she made up for with aggressiveness, attitude, and ass. Ris was the pursuer in our situation. I would get out of class and find flowers on my bed, or a jacket I'd been looking at in the mall would suddenly appear in my closet. I'd felt so betrayed and so hurt by what Rah did that for once I let my guard down and appreciated being cared for by another person.

I'll never forget our first time together. We were both drunk on our asses, lying on the floor, watching *Love & Basketball*. Ris was telling me about how she used to be obsessed with Sanaa Lathan and thought I looked just like her. One minute I was hysterically laughing my ass off, only to find myself torn between slapping the shit out of Ris and confused as to why my body was reacting like a jolt of electricity was surging through me from the feel of her lips on mine. For the first time in my life, I was made love to. Drunk or not, no man had ever made me feel the way Ris made me feel.

If I allowed myself to consider the notion of settling down with a woman, she fit every preconceived image of everything I'd ever wanted. She was great with Trey, treated me like a queen, and had such a free spirit. It hurt me to my core to see her right now, looking defeated with tears running silently down her cheeks. All because I hadn't come to grips with my own sexuality or learned to identify my true self. When it's all said and done, I'd never been with anyone but Rasheed or Larissa. I set my glass on the coffee table and took her hand.

"Well, since you asked me, I guess I'm gonna have to take your last name, huh?" I smiled through my tears and sniffled as her eyes widened in surprise and I continued, "Mrs. Larissa Roberts . . . I think Mrs. Michelle Roberts sounds like a pretty decent name for a VP, don't you?"

We'd probably have to go to California or something to make it legit, but my mind was made up and I was willing to do whatever it'd take to make Ris happy.

# Caged Birds

## 28

Four fuckin' puke-pink walls. For the last two weeks I'd been stuck in this damn cell starin' at four fuckin' puke-pink walls. I was bein' held without bail in bullshit-ass Fairview County Jail, and couldn't find a decent lawyer anywhere who was willin' to represent me. From what I could get outta T, forensics matched the bullets they took outta li'l Rasheed and Derrick back to a .45 registered in my name.

I couldn't get to Big Baby to find out what the fuck was goin' on but I only had one .45 and it stayed locked up in my office. It was obvious to me I was bein' set the fuck up. I'd been tryin'a hit Michelle with no luck, and really needed to figure out how the hell I was gonna tell her I had a daughter I needed her to take care of until this shit was sorted out. They were still tryin'a locate Honey's next of kin so, in the mean time, Paris was in foster care. It killed me knowin' I had a li'l girl out there bein' raised by some random-ass nigga. I slammed my head back against the cell wall in frustration. How the fuck did shit come to this?

I was certain the district attorney was tryin'a set me up with these murder charges since Honey took the wrap on Inferno for me. I needed to get in contact with Michelle, but every time I tried her cell it went straight to voice mail and when I called the house she never picked up. I was sure this ain't what she needed on top of seein' me wit' Diamond, but I needed her right now. I needed to know Trey was okay. I really needed her insight, her guidance. She was always my go-to on the next best course of action I needed to take.

All this thinkin' was makin' me go insane. I got down on the filthy floor and started doin' pushups to burn some energy. *One. Two. Three. Four.*

"Yo, nigga."

I heard a voice from the cell beside mine, but ignored it. That nigga always wanted something. Toilet paper, matches, you name it. *Five. Six. Seven. Eight.*

"Yo, so I heard you da nigga dat was runnin' da Hot Spot—da nigga dat was puttin' out dat muthafuckin' Inferno. Ya let ya bitch take the wrap."

*Nine. Ten.* My shoulders were startin' to burn. I decided to humor dude and see what the fuck he had to say. "Yeah, an' if I was?" I didn't even break my rhythm.

"If you *was* that same muthafucka, I'd tell you that one of your bitches was lookin' into some filthy shit before all dem fien's was hit wit' death warrants." He paused. An officer walked by makin' the rounds before lights out.

"My fuckin' unk died from that bullshit like a month ago, autopsy say it was a fentanyl overdose. Shit like a hundred times stronger than morphine."

I started sweatin' but it wasn't from the pushups. I got up an' dusted off my hands.

"What the fuck you sayin', nigga?" I was startin' to get more agitated by the second.

"I'm sayin' unless you doin' some extra, unheard-of cuttin', somebody was deliberately fuckin' up yo' shit, nigga. Nobody use shit like that to cut up no muthafuckin' horse, nigga! I need to know who you was gettin' ya shit from. I got business to handle."

"Nigga, I already got shit handled, why the fuck you think I'm in here now?" He was startin' to piss me off. The last thing I needed was accusations, or more shit to link me to Inferno. Honey gave her life for me on that; as far as I was concerned the matter was handled.

"You might believe yo' shit square, B, but I was doin' some diggin' an' the one pharmacist mufucka who even sell that typ'a shit under the table out here told me he sold a lotta shit to some bitch jus' befo' all dem ODs started poppin' up all ova the news. Fuckin' shame I had to stick his pussy ass to get him to talk, mighta found out who the bitch was if the muthafucka ain't die first. I hope you got two charges 'gainst yo' ass, muthufucka, or somebody still out there sittin' free an' clear while you in here."

With that I heard him shuffle toward the opposite corner of his cell. I reluctantly sat down on the stiff, piss-smellin' bunk I was given and mulled over what he'd said. After all was said and done, was Honey workin' wit' Derrick? I replayed the last time I talked to D in my head and couldn't make ends meet. Michelle'd picked up the last drop. It took her forever but she said she had a flat. She had enough time to fuck my shit up if she wanted to. If she was fuckin' Derrick why would she keep meetin' him at the club like Big said? What if they were plannin' out shit and swappin' product? I didn't know if havin' nothing else to think 'bout was makin' me draw pointless conclusions or what, but suddenly there seemed to be an even greater fuckin' chance that Michelle could have been doin' more with Derrick than just fuckin'!

# Baby Mommas

## 29

I had the worst headache imaginable. This was exactly what the hell I was trying to avoid. I opened my eyes and could feel every painful thud of my heartbeat in my temples. My chest felt heavy and hot; Ris was sprawled across me, naked, her face beside mine, still snoring in my ear. For her to be so damn small she sure knew how to take up a lot of space. I closed my eyes and tried to remember specific events from the night before. They came to me in reverse. Ris sprawled out on her stomach, my face buried in her thick, full ass, licking every inch of her pussy from back to front. Tangling my fingers in her hair, tryin'a stop the room from spinning long enough to focus; legs up on her shoulders, begging her for Ike, our strap-on. I'd never seen one in my entire life until Ris brought Ike home a few months ago. It was longer, thicker, and blacker than anything I'd ever imagined.

Our first night was awkward; she'd never used one, and had to practice the whole thrusting motion that comes more naturally to men. She picked one that strapped between her legs instead of around her waist. This way it rubbed against her sensitive parts and the harder she fucked me the better it felt to us both. I'd never experienced that side of Ris, the demanding and domineering side. It was like she literally transformed into someone else, and Ike became more of an extension of herself than a toy. Ever since then we'd just decided to call it Ike. She'd strap up and playfully tease me, askin', "Is you ready to sang the song, Annie-Mae?" and of course I'd start sangin'.

My heart took a dive in my chest. *I'm engaged. To a woman!* I felt myself panic. Was I really going to go through with this? Did I want to raise my son in a home with two mommies? How would I explain this to him when he got older? Would the kids in school tease him because of me? I shifted and wrapped my arms around Ris, pulling her closer into me, and closed my eyes. I could count a hundred times that I'd lain on Rah's chest, or woken up beside him and, yet, not once did I ever feel as complete or as right as I felt right this second. We got along so well considering we were exact opposites. Ris was the loudmouth life of the party, center of attention, sexy and comfortable in her own skin. She naturally brought out the playful side of me. Ris made me forget about bank figures and contract negotiations, and with her I could focus on unwinding and living. I was raised by both my parents in the suburbs. They were strict, normal, and would never understand my current situation. Ris, on the other hand, was raised by her momma in Detroit; she was accustomed to struggle and poverty and they barely ever spoke to each other.

I sometimes felt like it was my job to erase all of the memories of never having enough by giving her everything she could possibly ever want. I liked men, she liked women . . . Okay, so I liked women too, and my relationship with Ris had its bumps, but it had still managed to evolve into a real relationship. She never liked Rasheed, and every time I came to her cryin' about some new bullshit he'd pulled, she did her best to help me get over him. She hated him so much for me. Maybe I should have felt guilty for my relationship with her. I should have probably been embarrassed or felt uneasy, but she had always given me what Rasheed couldn't—trust an' love.

My BlackBerry dinged on the nightstand. It was after 8:00 A.M. The first time Rah called me from the jail I'd marked the number to go straight to voice mail. My phone wouldn't ring when he called, I'd just get a notification. I wasn't ready to talk to his ass yet. I was still too angry to talk rationally with him but I needed to let him know how all of the cheating, lying, and bullshit made me into a bitter woman. Eventually, I was going to have to put all that aside and, finally, tell him why things had to be the way they were going to be. As much as I felt that he deserved exactly what he was getting, I was not looking forward to the conversation.

Something told me back when I found out about one of his other side chicks, Danita, I should have walked away and never looked back. It always hurt Ris so much every time I decided to go back to him, and I didn't know what I would do if I ever lost her for good. The worst part about using a person to rebound from being with someone else is that your heart is never completely available. Every time I tried to focus on Ris to get over the hurt from dealing with Rasheed, a part of me still longed for him. I hadn't seen or heard from Rah for nearly six months after the incident when Katrice stabbed him. I was pretty certain what she told me about him was the truth and I was doing everything in my power to get over him. One day, out of the blue, he texted to ask my advice on some business. One thing led to another and, even though he hadn't fully regained my trust, we got back together.

Everything seemed normal for the first few months. Back then me and Ris never called what we had a relationship. When I took Rah back she kind of just fell back in place as a good friend, no questions asked. It'd always been like that between us. She would act jealous and not speak to me for days at a time whenever I went home to visit or stayed the night at a hotel with him, but I looked at Ris as my so-called college experiment and I was quite certain that I just wasn't cut out to be a lesbian. I missed my daddy dick-downs entirely too much. That was way before Ris and I discovered the wonders of Ike.

When Rah and I had gotten back together he was the perfect gentleman, for a little while anyway. It wasn't until he started cancelling trips to come see me or not answering my calls late at night that I knew he was up to something. Everything Rah had ever had had always been in my name. His cars, his cell phones, even his Costco membership was under mine. He'd always kept his phone locked and glued to his side so I knew if I ever wanted to know anything I would need access to it. One day I was switchin' into a new cell and I learned that the old phone

I'd jus' taken off of my number could still receive every text even though it wasn't active. The guy in customer service told me it was called cloning. Even though the phone was inactive it could still receive texts an' voice mail notifications. That's why they always suggest you erase the memory or simply keep your old cell turned off whenever you get a new one. I bought a spare phone, called customer service, and put it on his line, sayin' his original phone was stolen, waited an hour, and then called back, sayin' we found the original. Sure enough a few minutes later a text came through on the cloned phone. I didn't recognize the number, but I was pretty sure it wasn't Derrick textin' to ask if Rah was "ready to tear up dis pussy." I blocked my number and called to confront the bitch on the other line. I got her voice mail on the first try. I listened to the recording, trying to picture the face that went along with the soft-spoken woman who was fuckin' my man. Did she look better than me? Was he in love with her? Why her, what did she have that would make him want her so much that he'd lie to me? I redialed her number, prepared to just leave her a damn message.

"Hello?" It was the voice from the voice mail.

I was shocked she'd answered. "Hi, um, I'm sure you don't know me, or even know about me but, um, I'm Rasheed's fiancée. I need to know what's up with y'all." I exaggerated a little, but fuck it. I wanted her to feel fucked up, I wanted her to hurt like I was hurting.

"Maybe I need to be askin' who the fuck you are, 'cause me an' Rah been together a minute now. He in my bed ere fuckin' night so I don't know when he got time to fuck wi'chu. I think you got the wrong person." Her tone became snappy, far from the soft, playful woman she presented on her voice mail.

"No, momma, I've got the right person. You just sent my man a text and I got it. I'm away at college but we've been together since high school. He runs the Hot Spot with his boy Derrick. I'm Michelle. Ask him 'bout me." And with that I disconnected the call. The ball was in her court. When Ris got in from class I told her what had transpired between myself and another one of Rah's side chicks.

"Shit, Michelle! Anotha one? How many bitches you gotta run into befo' you realize that nigga dirty?" She was agitated, pacing back and forth in front of me while I sat on my bed, teary-eyed, hugging one of his T-shirts I'd taken when I left for college.

"I don't know, girl. I mean he was my first love, my first boyfriend. We've got a lotta firsts. I helped him buy his first strip club. We're supposed to be building an empire together."

"*What about our firsts, Chelle? If all it take is a dick to make you feel happy then, fuck it, I'll go buy one! You deserve mo' than what that nigga willin' to give you, girl. Open ya eyes! Why do you keep fuckin' wit' him?*" she asked me.

"*I don't know, Ris, I'm sorry. I just don't know.*"

But I knew the answer. Call it what you want, sprung, turned out, it was what it was. The dick was better than good. Whenever me and Rah fought, we'd have that "I love you so much I hate you" makeup sex. The type of shit that starts as soon as you open the front door and ends with clothes spread from one side of the house to the other, pictures knocked off the wall, and furniture all out of place. Whenever Rah did anything wrong he used his dick to say sorry, and the more sorry he was the better it would be. At those times I didn't mind the biting or the roughness. I just wished that sometimes he would switch it up, be a little more gentle, or a little more romantic. Our makeup sex would always hit like a major earthquake, and what I'd done with Ris at the time was like a quiet, calm spring rain in comparison.

Everything was quiet for nearly a month after I spoke with Danita. Rah sent me flowers every day and apologies in the form of letters, cookies, you name it. Ris made it a point to throw away any- and everything he sent to our dorm. However, once again after relying on Ris to get me through I backslid, and it started with me checking his texts. Day to day, he was only getting texts about busi- ness from his boys. No new messages from Danita or any other girls ever came through on what I started callin' the Batphone.

Rah was being so attentive and apologetic. In a moment of weakness durin' spring break, Ris left to go see her family and I asked Rah to come talk to me. We were on each other before I could even close the door. We never talked out our problems; I never asked him for explanations, I'd just get my dick-down and then we'd fall back in sync as though nothing out of the ordinary had happened.

Rah was supposed to stay with me for the entire week of spring break but had to cut the trip short because of some sort of emergency. I'd hid the Batphone while he was in town. I went to check it after he'd left and was in tears by the time I'd finished reading texts from *her*. She was apologizing for accusing him of cheating and wanted him to come home. And he'd actually lied to my face and run off to go be with her. My phone rang and I answered without looking.

*"This is Michelle."* I could barely talk around the lump in my throat.

*"Hi. Michelle, this is Danita. Rasheed was jus' wit' you, wasn't he?"* She sounded exactly how I felt.

*"How did you get this number? And, yes, but he left—he said he had an emergency."* I sniffled loudly and tried to find something to wipe my nose with. I made the mistake of using one of his T-shirts from my laundry pile; new tears welled up as I inhaled Issey Miyake and cried loudly into the phone.

*"Michelle, I confronted Rasheed that night you called and I asked him who you were. He got so damn angry an' defensive. He said you weren't nobody an' you ain't mean shit to him. He gave me your number an' told me to call you an' ask you myself if y'all were fuckin' or not. He ain't think I would actually ever call you I guess."*

It felt like my heart had been split in half. I didn't have anything to say to her. She continued.

*"I was calling to let you know I think I'm pregnant an' I ain't have anyone else to talk to. I called Rahsheed but he wouldn't answer. But his bitch ass responded to all my texts. I knew somethin' was up. I really need to thank you*

*for tellin' me 'bout his dawg ass. Girl, dat nigga doesn't deserve either of us, an' I know he's been lyin' to me. All the times he's been wit' me when his phone rings an' he won't answer it. It stays locked an' he even takes it in the bathroom wit' him. What kinda shit is that? Michelle, I'm done. No nigga's worth my tears."*

We talked for quite some time. For all the months they were together she just knew he was being one hundred with her. I thought Danita was more upset than I was. It's hard to be in love with a nigga when you *know* he's doing you wrong. Love makes us forgive everything and fall for damn near anything. It's fucked up that a person can cause you so much pain and still be the only one in the world who can make the hurt go away.

If Danita hadn't known about me, she might have considered keeping the baby, but she couldn't stand the thought of havin' to deal with Rah for the next eighteen years. She didn't know any other way to make money if she couldn't dance at the club. She'd told me she was getting rid of it. As much as I hated her for sharin' my man, as a woman and a mother, I would never have wished what Rasheed did to her.

All of this I told to Ris. I told her everything, always had.

*"So, now you know he ain' fuckin' wit' ol' girl, you gonna take him back again, huh?"* She wasn't even mad that he'd been in our room during spring break, or that once again she was probably going to end up being on the back burner while I tried to make Rah love me the way I felt I deserved to be loved.

*"Momma, I don't know what to do. Why ain't I enough for him? All the shit I do for him and put up with, why does he keep looking at other bitches? It feels like I can't win."* I was getting frustrated and my self-esteem was slowly deteriorating.

*"Look, baby, if you gonna keep fuckin' wit' his bitch ass da least you can do is make bank off da muthafucka, damn!"*

Ris had never been more right or made more sense. We hugged and made the decision to change our lives for the better. No matter what, we were going to eat and live the lavish life off that nigga and that, in itself, would compensate for all the bullshit I'd been putting up with. I even managed to keep in touch with Danita and, when she got locked up, I was the one who suggested she send li'l Rah to stay with us. It was time Rah learned about his son anyway. I would have never guessed, not in a million years, that Rah's jealousy would get the best of him to the degree that he'd actually put a child in danger.

I'd told Danita a hundred times she needed to tell Rah about his son. Deep down I thought what she wanted was to mete out some kind of silent revenge for what he'd done to her face and her life. I thought about Trey and couldn't even begin to imagine the kind of pain she must have been going through right now.

"I can hear yo' ass thinkin'. Them wheels spinnin' so loud they woke me up." Ris kissed me on my cheek, stretched, and yawned. "What are you thinkin' 'bout, baby?"

She rolled off of my chest and stretched out on her side, facing me. She lightly trailed her fingertips along the arches of my eyebrows.

"You worry way too much. Black don't crack, but you damn sure tryin'a put some creases up here. If you gonna be Mrs. Roberts, we gotta preserve these good looks. I can't have everyone thinkin' you my momma an' not my wife when we go to Pride nex' year!" She giggled.

I balked. I had no intention of attending any kind of gay pride celebrations, but I'd have to break that to Ris at another time.

"Ris, we the same age, stop playin'. I have to worry for all of us. Our web is big, bigger than I'd expected, and we need to make sure all of the flies that get tangled in it are wrapped up tight." I knew that was probably over her head but it's the best way I could explain our situation. The more complex things got the more people we had to get involved, and if we weren't careful it would only take one slip and everything would go completely to shit. I needed to make sure every angle was covered from every direction, every viewpoint, down to every single detail.

I leaned up and kissed Ris on the forehead. "Okay, this is the last time. I promise. Tell me how much we can trust Shiree on this one? If anything gets out, shit can get real hot for us both, real fast." I was confident that with all the drug money and all my legit money we could pull this off. But everyone had to play their part, follow their scripts, and if anything switched up we needed to improvise accordingly.

Never in a million years would I have ever guessed Ris's li'l sister Shiree, aka Big Shirley, would end up messin' with Big Baby and gettin' burned. I didn't see it comin', but I sure as hell saw it as a solution.

# Still Waters Run Deep

## 30

Everything had fallen into place just as I'd hoped, if not better. I had Ris's reassurance that Shiree would stay in pocket and, since we'd paid her at least three times what she normally saw in a year from dancing at the club, I finally felt more confident in my plan. Things were fitting together flawlessly. I wasn't sure if it was blind luck or fate, but I never would have thought the day Ris moved her cousin in would be the day to change all of our lives.

If there's one thing I had to give Rah credit for, it would definitely be his financial support. Dealing with Rah on a personal level had me accustomed to being home alone and often. He may have never been there, but he sure as hell made sure everything was paid on time. All of our bills were paid in full, the house was paid off, and all the cars. I was the go-to person at the bank, and

my salary was almost $100,000 a year. Thanks
to Rah I rarely needed to touch my own money.
I invested most of it and paid for Larissa's home.
If Rasheed had had any idea how much my
net worth really was, I doubted he'd have ever
stepped a foot back out on the streets to hustle.

Trenisha, aka Honey, was Ris's nineteen-
year-old first cousin. She was livin' with their
grandmother and basically runnin' wild, losin'
her damn mind. When she almost died from an
OxyContin overdose, she was sent to Larissa's.
Their grandmother swore up and down the girl
was tryin' to kill herself, but I know a little about
recreational drug use and it just seemed to be
something that ran deep in that family. Don't get
me wrong, Larissa was my heart, but she'd always been the type of person to look for different
kinds of highs. It started with liquor in college.
Then she started smoking weed, popping ec-
tasy, and when I got pregnant with Trey, Larissa
started doin' coke and Lord knew what else. She's
always tried to hide her drug use from me but I'd
accepted her for who she was, flaws and all. Hell,
half the niggas out there worked for Rah. Even
though they didn't know Ris was my girlfriend,
it bothered me to have her out buying shit off of
the street like that. When needed, I could bypass
Rasheed and talk Derrick into sellin' me what I

needed to keep her out of trouble but, no matter how much I gave her, it was never enough. I put a lot of the blame on myself since I couldn't be with her full time. I asked her once if she could quit all the drugs for me and she told me if she had me full time she wouldn't need a high to feel good. I did that for her.

I tried putting myself in her shoes a thousand times and if the shoe was on the other foot and she was the one bouncing between me and another nigga, I would have cut her loose a long time ago. I knew I had to have been puttin' her through hell. She loved me so much an' had always tried so hard to understand my relationship wit' Rah. I encouraged her to date other women, go out and meet new people, but she always refused. Telling me that I was enough for her and one day I'd realize she was enough for me. I didn't think I'd ever be able to love a man the same way that I love her. It's hard to explain the difference between being in love with a man and loving another woman. One is empathetic and understanding, the other can be protective and domineering. I was torn between whether I want to be dominated or be dominating.

The way Rah provided for me was the way I provide for Ris. She didn't have to work or worry about money because I took care of all that. I started a stay-at-home business for her a year ago, specializing in sex toys, lubes, you name it, but having Honey come stay at the house didn't make matters any better. Ris suggested she audition and dance at the club since she was young and didn't want to seriously hold a regular job, plus she would be under the watchful eye of Shiree to make sure she stayed out of trouble. I wanted no part in that shit. That was one side of the business Rah seemed to never have a problem running by himself. Of course, Honey auditioned and got the job; she was thick, pretty, and a little too hoodish for my standards but just right for the club.

It didn't take long before Ris and Honey started combining whatever she earned at the club with Ris's profits from the business and they'd waste it on pills, alcohol, and whatever else. I was helping Ris with a romance party one night when Honey wandered in right in the middle of my "good head" demonstration. Thankfully, we didn't have a huge turnout that night; there were only two couples and a few women from my job gathered in our living room.

*"Oh, girl, I need som'a dat for my boo!" She burst into the room wearing what looked like a black spandex cat suit minus the tail, breasts pushed up so high they touched her chin, and she was obviously high as hell.*

*I was annoyed. I couldn't believe she'd just interrupted me during a presentation.*

*"Honey, what boo you talking about?" I asked. "You either working at the club or you're here with Ris. Let me find out y'all kissin' cousins." I smirked, proud of how quickly I'd cut her down, and repositioned myself to finish demonstrating to my clients the best angle to deep throat using a banana.*

*"Shiiit, well, I guess you can say I puts in a li'l ova time wit' the boss, an' um' his fine yella ass pays a bitch bills, so I needs to know how to work him so he drop mo' of dat serious paper." She was two-steppin' in place like she'd won the lottery and cheesin' at me like the cat that ate the canary.*

*I gagged despite the glob of numbing cream dabbed in the back of my throat and my audience stared on in surprise.*

*It's ironic that neither I nor Ris bothered to tell Honey that fine-ass "yella nigga" running the Hot Spot was already taken. It never even crossed my mind to mention it. Maybe somewhere deep down I really wanted Rasheed to fuck up, maybe I just really wanted a reason to finally live my life the way I felt I should be living it. I fought to hide my reaction and avoided making eye contact with Ris, who was giving me an "I told you so" glare. Honey and the rest of our guests were waiting for me to continue with my demonstration, but I was just too shocked and growing even more upset by the second. Ris saved me from embarrassing myself and took over while I went upstairs to cool off.*

*"Sorry, y'all. Okay. Ladies, rule number one is that you gotta remember to breathe through ya nose when . . ." Ris's words trailed off as I left the room.*

That was it, I was done feeling sorry for myself. Years ago Ris and I had decided Rah would fund our futures, whether he wanted to or not, and at that moment I'd felt that enough had been done to secure our well-being and everything had advanced to the point where we no longer needed him in the picture.

# Questions

## 31

Today was the day. Michelle had finally agreed to come see a nigga! I'd been dreamin' 'bout her, damn near goin' crazy in here tryin' to figure out what she been doin' or if she been fuckin' somebody else already. I had so much shit to say an' ain't even know where to start. I ain't neva felt so fucked up in all my life. I had to watch my momma break down at my sentencing. She acted like they was givin' my ass the death sentence or some shit, but consecutive life sentences is damn close enough I guess. I was appealin' my sentence 'cause even though my gun was used in the murders that was all the fuck they had to convict me. When it's all said an' done there wasn't enough circumstantial evidence, an' talkin' to a few niggas in here made me think I had a chance at callin' it a mistrial. I'd asked Chelle not to bring Trey up here. I didn't really

want him to see me like this, an' even though I
know he wouldn't understand now, I jus' prayed
as he got older he would one day understand
why I hustled an' why he needed to make betta
decisions than I had.

This prison shit ain't no fuckin' cakewalk.
Yeah, I had connects from my boys outside an' a
few of the guards in here used to be on my roster,
but they could only do so much. For the most
part a nigga could still get real food, pussy, and
my card stayed loaded up wit' cash regardless of
me needin' shit or not. I needed to know Chelle
was gonna support a nigga; until my appeal went
through, I needed to make sure she kept my shit
in play on the streets and kept the cash flow on
point so we would stay set. She didn't come to
my trial and I didn't want her to. It was important that she not appear to have anything to do
with the bullshit I was in. It hurt to sit in front
of the judge and have my momma sit and cry as
I was handed my sentence, but I pushed all that
shit down inside me and ignored the pain and
the anger.

"Inmate, at attention."

One of the guards was glarin' at me from outside my cell. I'd nicknamed his bitch ass "Baby
Shit." He one of them niggas who played like
they hard than a mufucka, but really he softer

than baby shit. He was one of the few niggas who gave me grief over my special treatment, but he couldn't do shit about it. He was kinda new and still tryin'a get in where the fuck he fit in with the otha guards. It ain' take much to realize they had they own social hierarchy in here. A guard who wasn't down was a liability, and they salary wasn't shit so they made bank off niggas like me.

"You know the routine, nigga, solitary."

I turned my back and put my hands up to the space in the cell bars behind me. He roughly snapped the cold metal cuffs around my wrists behind my back and then shackled my ankles.

"We need to make this shit quick, my baby momma comin' to see me today." I was led out of my cell and down a flight of stairs toward the solitary confinement cells. The entire ambiance changes when you hit solitary. The hallway is dim and most of the lights in the ceiling are either out or flickerin'. The entire wing was designated for high risk, violent, and hard-to-manage inmates. I, however, was none of these.

"A'ight, nigga, Officer Reynolds got you for the next hour." Baby Shit led me toward the last cell at the end of the hall and knocked twice before unlockin' the door and nudgin' me inside.

"Took you long enough to get down here, nigga, you know I don't like to wait."

I tried to wait for my eyes to adjust but couldn't make out anything in the pitch-black cell. It smelled like bleach, piss, and old body sweat; solitary always smelled that way. I closed my eyes and inhaled slowly. Cool Water for Women drifted toward me. It was not one of my favorite fragrances but I shuffled in the direction of the perfume anyway.

"I heard ya baby momma comin' today so I decided to get you in here early. Don't want that dick standin' at attention for nobody but me. Ya hear me, nigga?"

I could hear her moving toward me from the opposite side of the cell. She struck a match, lightin' the room up jus' long enough for me to see her as she stopped in front of me, naked, her uniform crumpled in the corner.

"You know this yo' dick, baby. I ain't pressed 'bout seein' that bitch; she ain't made it stand up in years. I jus' need to make sure she keep my paper right an' take care of my son." Like I said, a nigga still get pussy, even on lockdown. Officer Reynolds wasn't a five star, first class, hell she wasn't even back-up material. There was nothin' cute on or about her, but when it's dark, pussy feel like pussy, ya hear me. She was far from the usual type of woman I fucked wit', but it was this or my hand 'cause I wasn't lettin' anotha nigga suck me off. We usually met up in the evenin's.

We were let outta our cells twice a week to see this bullshit psychiatrist. I ain't neva met the nigga personally, but he sure as hell expensive than a mufucka. Cost me thirty thou jus' to get him to keep his mouth shut and another ten Gs to write up false observations and shit like he been seein' me on a regular basis. I was cool with him, but shrinks didn't last long in here. If we got anotha one anytime soon the price would probably go up and I would be outta money if I had to keep doin' this kind of shit. My sanity in here depended on whether or not I could get Chelle to do some work for me on the outside to keep our cash flow up.

One of my boys told me 'bout her sellin' the club and shit so she was def' stackin' paper. The few who were still loyal to me had finished off the last of their sales and had been puttin' the cash on the books for me in here. Without the lights on I could pretend her lips were Michelle's, or Diamond's, or even Honey's. Yeah, it would be real good to see Chelle.

# Princes and Princesses

## 32

I looked out over the city from my office on the eighteenth floor. You could smell the spring fever. It was finally starting to stay light outside longer and we were sitting in the lower sixties almost every day. The sun glimmered off the diamond on my left hand, drawing my attention downward. Four months ago, I'd become engaged to Ris. She loved me and made love to me in ways Rasheed would never be able to or ever even wanted to. She was such a romantic and always so gentle, touching me the right way, kissing me just the way I liked. Rah was always on some grab, bite, and pull rough porno shit. It was starting to become clear that Ris was the perfect balance for me. I never knew it was physically possible to be in love with two different people at the same time. But there I was. I loved them both for very different reasons and I finally got the courage to face the reality of making up my mind.

Rah'd been charged with double homicide and was sentenced to consecutive life sentences and I was living as close to a perfect life as I possibly could. It was still early. If I changed my mind and never showed up Rah wouldn't be able to do shit about it. I'd finally spoken with him and agreed to visit him today. It wouldn't be easy but I needed this face-to-face time. I finally needed closure.

I had one stop to make before I headed to the penitentiary to see Rasheed. In the beginning I'd planned to just leave Rasheed and take his money with me. Derrick was always loyal to Rah; there was no need for him to go as far as he went and justice had been served in this instance. When I'd told Rah about the fraud situation I'd handled at the bank, I was certain he'd try it. He was always looking for ways to hide or move money. I'd started a credit watch program with Equifax the week before telling him the bank idea, and sure enough when First Union ran my info to open an account I was immediately sent a confirmation e-mail to activity under my Social Security number. I contacted one of my girls who was a teller at the bank, and she had no problem giving me the account number and the balance.

It was in my name after all. Over the course of the last six months or so Rasheed had been conducting business and telling whoever to deposit shit they owed him there or put it on his books. He had over $200,000 in that checking account alone. I planned to withdraw it all and close the account for good.

My phone chimed, letting me know I had an appointment scheduled in my calendar. I checked my reflection in the mirror. I'd chosen to wear my hair loose the way he liked it, and the forty-five minutes a day on the stair climber in our corporate gym had my ass and hips fitting nicely into my black and grey Lanvin blazer and matching skirt; both gifts from Ris. I admired my skin and my cheekbones in the glass. I looked well rested and happy for a change. I'd been quietly liquidating most of Rasheed's assets. All of the cars minus the S-class Benz were sold; I'd given that to Ris since she always admired it. I'd sold the Hot Spot, the house, anything that ever connected Rasheed's life to mine was gone. I called to check on Ris.

"Hey, Chelly Bean."

"Hey, baby. How is our li'l princess?" I was referring to Lataya, Trenisha's daughter. Trenisha was only given a 10 percent chance at surviving and was pretty much being kept alive by the machines they had her hooked up to. The primary options for her daughter were to go to her grandmother, who wanted nothing to do with the baby, a foster home, or stay here with us since, after all, Ris was still her family. I'd always wanted another child, and since we were starting our lives together, Larissa surprised me when she was the one who said it was only fair that we give the product of all our sins a better chance at life.

"She's finally 'sleep! I don't know how you did this shit, I don't think I'm cut out to be a momma. It's kickin' my ass." She sounded dead tired and my heart went out to her. When I was going through that stage with Trey, Rah was in the club almost every night and it felt like I was always tired, always alone, and at the mercy of Trey's temperament.

"Aww, baby, you're doin' fine. I swear all new mommas go through it. You're getting better at it, I promise."

"Yeah, but all new mommas don't have babies who can't stand they asses. I jus' know that li'l heffa saves all the poops, fusses, an' messes for me!" Ris was dead certain the baby couldn't stand her because she'd cry and fuss the entire time she was with her. It was the exact opposite with me; she'd coo and make all the wonderful baby sounds that I remembered enjoying with

Trey and then she'd be off to sleep. I saw so much of Rah when I looked at her little face: his defiant sharp chin, and narrow nose. She was exactly my complexion and so chubby with kissable fat rolls everywhere, I called her my Michelin Tire baby. It was easy adjusting to her in the house since Ris was pretty much a stay-at-home mommy. I'd even jokingly started calling her my baby momma.

"I'll be home in a little bit. I've got something for you. Maybe it'll make you feel better."

"Yeah, you've got somethin' that'll make me feel better all right. I'm goin' to take my ass a shower while everything's calm."

Ris rushed off the phone and I put my things into my Louis Vuitton laptop bag. It was time to face down my demon. I said a silent prayer for strength, guidance, and protection. Yes, I was definitely going to be needing all three since I had no idea how Rasheed would react to finally learning the truth about everything

# Just Start at the Beginning

## 33

I'd never visited anyone in prison before. This was going to be harder than I thought. I signed in and was led to the non-contact visit area. Since Rah and I weren't married and I wasn't immediate family, I was not allowed to physically be in the same space as him. This was fine by me. I had a pretty good feeling after I told Rah everything I needed to tell him that it would be in my best interest to have a thick glass wall between us.

The other side of the room was stark grey. Nothing was present except for the phone on the side of the wall directly across from the phone beside me. I expected to feel remorse or unhappiness. The door opened and Rah was led in by an intimidating mannish-looking woman. She eyed me from behind him as he sat at the bench looking as attractive as the day I'd first met him. He'd put on some muscle and let his beard grow out, giving him a rugged, dangerous appeal. He waited until she left the room an' picked up the phone. I did the same.

"Michelle, baby. You don't know how happy I am to see you." He sighed, and looked at me expectantly as if he were waiting for me to say the same. I wanted to tell him what he expected, take the easy way out and leave him in there thinkin' everything would be fine.

"I'm sorry you gotta see me like this, Chelle. I fucked up—I know. I jus' need to know you gonna try to wait for a nigga. I love you, baby. I really do."

"Well, Rasheed, that seems to be something you pretty good at. Fuckin' up, that is." I couldn't hide my anger. I'd had to listen to him say he'd fucked up or he's sorry for so many years. *Fuck Rasheed.* Before he could reply or I lost my nerve I continued.

"I have a confession to make, because none of this shit would have ever started if you would have just been the man I needed you to be. Shit. Rasheed, you could have just told me the truth, been honest with everything, and we would have been fine."

He stared at me, about to argue, but I had to get this over with. I was ready to start my life with Larissa and leave all this drama and bullshit behind me.

"The day you decided to fuck Trenisha—I'm sorry, I mean Honey—and lie to me was the day you fucked up your shit for good. Who the fuck you think talked her ass into getting a cell phone, Rasheed? Hell, I took her to buy it. All those nights y'all were together, who you think she was talking to, nigga? Do you know how it made me feel to hear this bitch talking about how good her nigga, my nigga, was dickin' her down?" I was getting riled up and had to watch my tone. I needed to compose myself. Rah must have thought I needed an explanation or what I liked to call a plausible lie.

"Chelle, listen to me. You know how those stripper hoes get down. Whateva she said I swear it wasn't like that, ba—"

"Rasheed, who do you think Honey was livin' with? When she told us you bought her a car I was mortified. I couldn't believe you would do something like that to me. To us. When I wasn't sure if she was exaggerating I checked your phone, nigga."

His eyes widened. He wasn't expecting that.

"No, I don't know your lock code if that's what you're thinking. But just as I expected you a grimy-ass nigga and you got some grimy-ass, oily-ass fingers. All I had to do was hold the phone up to the light and I could see the pattern you used for your unlock screen. I've read everything you ain't want me to read. I've seen everything you ain't want me to see. I've meant nothing to you. I can't believe you would stoop so low as to do what you did to a nigga you called your brother. Why? Because you were jealous that I was doing what you've always done?

"I wasn't even fuckin' Derrick. Honey was— dumbass! The only times I talked to that nigga or met up with him was when I needed to buy shit for Honey's cousin or when he couldn't find a re-up nigga for product and wanted to go through my connect. Yes, Rah, I have connects. I have a lotta shit you don't know about."

I needed to make this quick. Rah was starin' at me like he'd seen a ghost. The blood had rushed to his face; whether it was from anger or surprise I wasn't sure. His knuckles had turned white from gripping the phone so tightly. His other hand was clenched into a fist on the counter in front of him. I could tell he was trying to figure out if what I was saying was really what the hell he thought I was saying.

"You actually know my girlfriend, Rah. Y'all met once or twice. I think you might recall a certain someone comin' into your office and running off with that box of bullshit you keep in your desk?"

"You was cool wit' Honey's crackhead cousin? The one who was takin' all her fuckin' money an' . . ." He interrupted me, too shocked to even realize he wasn't denying his situation with Honey anymore.

"We're engaged, Rasheed, and Larissa ain't a crackhead. She never stole anything from Honey. Honey had been lying to you. They both like to do a little of this and a little of that but Honey's money was spent exactly the way she wanted to spend it. The only reason Larissa came to your office that night was because she was upset by what you'd done to me again, and again, and again. I have someone who loves me so much, she was willing to risk everything just to wipe your miserable ass off the planet. That's a million times more love than you've ever shown me!" I could feel the tears. My wounds ran so deep and now that I was telling the person who caused them I couldn't help feeling overwhelmed that the pain seemed so fresh. I prayed they didn't listen in on these conversations because I needed to get everything off my chest. I took a tissue from my purse and dabbed my eyes. I could no longer make eye contact with this man, liar, cheater, and my son's father. I stared down at my lap.

"Larissa is my girlfriend, Rasheed. She came there that night to kill you. When you left she decided to rob you instead, but all the drawers on your desk were locked except one."

Afraid to look up, I heard him draw in a sharp breath. "I didn't know she'd taken it, Rah. I swear. When Ris gets high she does stupid, stupid shit sometimes. I told her to get rid of it but for whatever reason she gave it to her sister, Shiree."

If the phone weren't in a death grip against my ear I never would have heard it, but he whispered, "Big Shirley, Shiree from the club?"

"Yes, Shiree was trying to make extra money and she sold it to Big Baby. She didn't know where it came from, all she knew is her sister had it for her to sell. The only people to ever touch it barehanded were you and Big Baby. He was stupid for lettin' those kids use it, but you were even dumber for puttin' that money out on D like that."

The phone was silent on my ear. I couldn't even hear him breathing. I looked up but Rah's head was in his hand and his eyes were closed. He was so still he looked like a stone carving. Being that I was the cause of his angst and despair, I could think of no better name for my work of art than *Torment*.

"Why would you even go through with something like that, Rah? You knew he had RJ with him."

His head shot up so quickly I swore I heard a snap, and we locked eyes. It was like he'd been transformed. I could see the anger, confusion, and the hurt all etched deeply into his face. His eyes were bloodshot, but still he didn't say a word.

"Yeah, I knew about Rasheed Jr. I've known his mother just as long as you have. I gave Danita my word that sending him to us would be a good idea, and I'd hoped that raising two little boys would help you finally realize that you were a grown-ass man. You too old to be pulling the same bullshit you been pulling since high school, Rah! I figured if I sabotaged your supply maybe you would start to consider other business ideas. In my eyes taking out one or two fiends was a valid price to pay if it got you to stop dealin'."

If we were side by side I'd be dead, his eyes told me that. I'd single-handedly destroyed Rasheed's life and, in his mind, I alone was the reason he was sitting on the other side of that glass and not out in the streets.

"I prayed that you would quit all that bullshit. The one thing I wanted out of everything in this world was for you, me, and Trey to be a family, a real family, Rah. Derrick was having a hard time finding product and didn't want to disappoint you. He looked up to you. I went to my connect to help him just as I'd done any other time, except this time I laced half of what I gave him. But that wasn't even enough for you to stop. When you sent me to get the next drop, I laced it all. Ris is the one who called the cops when you gave Honey that car. She was so jealous of Honey and the girl kept rubbing it in her face. It was obvious to us both that you were using her and I'm sure Honey didn't know anything about you and your cars. When Ris told me she'd called the police I just knew that with most of your product missing and the cops looking at things extra closely you would give up. My intentions were always good, Rasheed. I swear."

"Good? You think this shit is good? Look at where the fuck I am, Michelle, and all for what? Your pride? 'Cause you ain't woman enough to accept that a nigga dick like a li'l variety. You did all this shit ova some side-ass ho?"

I'd never forget the look on his face. He had angry tears in his eyes and I could imagine he felt somewhat akin to how kids feel when they realize you've lied about Santa or the Tooth Fairy. He was seeing firsthand the kind of damage that heartache can lead a woman to create. I only had one last thing to tell him.

"Don't worry, Rasheed. Trey will never have to do what his daddy did. In my opinion he don't even need to know his daddy. What the fuck is his daddy gonna teach him about being a man?"

His mouth opened and closed like a fish gulping for air. I knew he had so many questions and his hustler's mind was probably trying to form so many variations of whatever lie he felt would work best. I didn't plan on giving him the chance to have his say. He'd had years of saying, lying, embellishing.

"That account you and your li'l bitch opened up is in my name just like every other asset you've ever acquired. I'm taking it and we're moving. Banks don't like fraud and, as the new acting vice president, it didn't take much talking to convince your bank that I had power of attorney and wanted to close out all of your personal accounts as well. I loved you more than I loved myself. I saw more potential in you than you saw in you and I just can't be in love with that lie anymore. Take care, Rasheed."

I hung up the phone and for a second I looked into the cold, callous soul of a man I'd given so much to. I searched for the man I'd fallen in love with and realized I may have only imagined the compassionate and caring being I was so enamored with because, at the moment, it was nowhere before me.

His eyes had reddened and in a burst of rage he slammed the phone against the plexiglass window.

I fought to keep my composure and reassured myself that what I was doing was my best option for survival. The veins in his neck and forehead protruded painfully. It was like watching a silent movie as he began his violent tirade around the small enclosure. I jumped slightly as his foot landed against the thick plastic window in a loud thud and he screamed what I could only imagine were curses of hatred and the horrors of what he was going to have done to me.

Nostrils flared, saliva hanging from his mouth. In his rage he looked less like a man and more like the demon my mind had conjured him up to be. Two uniformed officers stormed into the room and tried to restrain him. I turned and left as Rasheed was violently slammed to the floor after punching the guard in the face. I didn't even bother looking back.

I was finally closing a chapter of my life that had been read and reread to such an extent that all the words looked the same, all the characters were predictable, and none of the endings were ones I wanted to be mine. Lovin' these niggas is hard work. They fuck up, and then we cry about it and argue over it. Eventually we either move forward with them or move on without 'em. It gets even more drawn out and more complicated when we have these niggas' babies.

My problem was that I'd always loved Rasheed. Rasheed's just the type of nigga who wouldn't eva love anyone more than he loved his damn self. It's sad that it took me this long to finally realize it. It wasn't fair that I'd been with this same nigga since I was sixteen, and here I was eight years and one baby later, nowhere near married to him and still putting up with the same shit over an' over again. After all the disrespect and the lying I was finally over it. I guess you can say that I was finally over being his crutch and his support but not being worthy enough to be his wife. I guess I finally got fed up with being nothing more than his baby momma.

# Puppet Masters

## 34

Let me make one thang clear to y'all: no matter what course of action ya take, there's somethin' that influences or affects the reason ya make ya final decisions. See, I was a needy bitch. I needed nice clothes, a nice car, hell, I needed all that finer shit these broke niggas hated on 'cause they couldn't an' neva would be able to afford it for they damn selves let alone give it to my ass. Shit, Larissa Roberts is a trophy muthafuckin' wife. I ain't workin' no damn five days a week at some bullshit-ass, eighty hour a pay period job jus' to make barely enough to pay my bills. My baby momma did all that an' then some. Chelly been mine ever since the day we met in college. It mighta took me a li'l while to get her to open up, but straight bitches don't stare at my ass daydreamin'! Somethin' told me from the jump she was "fam," an' my gaydar ain' neva been off. I ain't even mad at bein' stuck with Nisha's brat. If my baby wanted a big family then that's what the fuck my baby was gonna have. I can't lie though, I did want it to be our baby, but I guess if you took her ex-man and my cousin then Lataya was as much ours as she could ever be.

Speakin' of the devil. I got up from the couch and rushed to give Chelle kisses as she walked through the door.

"I gotta tip my hat to you, baby, you one of da smartest money-makin' bitches I know and I seen that shit from day one." It was true too; any nigga she decided to fuck wit' was gonna end up bein' a rich muthafucka if she had any say about it. Why she got so hung up on Rasheed's bum ho'n ass I didn't know. But I was glad I was finally able to split dat bullshit up.

"Mmm, hmm. You're just trying to butter me up because I brought you a present, right? I'm not fooled. Where are my babies?"

She looked past me an' sat down on the couch to take off her heels. I sat on the floor in front of her, as was our custom, an' massaged her left foot until I felt da muscles relax, an' did the same to her right.

"The baby is 'sleep an' Trey is in his room watchin' cartoons. Relax, ma." I ain't bother tellin' her my grandma had called an' cussed me

out for not lookin' after Nisha. I thought I'd feel
bad but I ain't never like Nisha's ass no damn
way. Da bitch got on my last nerve. I thought we
was cool 'til I found out she was fuckin' my ex-
girlfriend. I was sure niggas got all googly-eyed
thinkin' dey was gettin' into some virgin-type
pussy since she was young an' ain' neva fucked
wit' a lotta dudes. Shit! Dat's only 'cause she
been lickin' pussy since day muthafuckin' one!

When Trenisha broke down an' hit me for a
place to stay, da first thing I worried 'bout was
whether her ass was gonna try to press up on
Chelle. She gave me dis whole "I'm straight now"
song an' dance an' I had to give myself some
points for showin' a li'l mercy an' takin' her in.
Puttin' her in Rah's path was exactly what Michelle needed in order to see dat nigga wasn't eva
gonna change. Not fa himself, not fa his son, and
damn sure not fa Michelle's ass.

"What the hell you do now?"

Chelle was watchin' me intently. I'd jus' spaced
out on her for a sec, lost in my thoughts. "Damn,
baby, I ain' did shit. I was jus' thinkin' nothin' serious. Can I please have dis damn surprise now,
Chelle?" She laughed. Dis was torture an' she
knew it. I sat back on my haunches an' waited as
she opened her Louis laptop bag an' pulled out
a folder. My heart was doin' fuckin' flips in my

chest as I flipped it open, anxious to see what she'd done. For da first time in my life I cried what I'd heard bitches on TV call "tears of joy." Da first sheet of paper was a marriage license an' da second was a deed for . . . I skimmed over dat bitch as best as I could through my tears. Seven bedrooms, state-of-the-art appliances, $500,000, and Florida were the only words I could make out before I just all-out bawled like my ass was tryin'a steal da award from Lataya. Chelle was smilin' an' had started cryin' as she slid down onto the floor beside me.

"Larissa, you've been with me through everything, and I know I tell you how much you mean to me every day. Now I can finally start showing you, baby. For every tear I've made you cry and every bruise I've dealt your heart, I'm not gonna rest until I've replaced every single bad memory with fifteen good ones. Even if it takes every day. Until the day I die. This I promise."

We shared a genuine heartfelt kiss dat immediately turned lustful an' had me ready to go pull Ike da fuck out an' give her a serious-ass appreciation fuck. As if on cue, Lataya started whalin' an' we both laughed. Chelle stood up, smoothin' her skirt out an' straightenin' her hair as if she were worried that the baby would be able to tell we were just foolin' around.

"I'll go see to our princess an' make sure Trey isn't up there deconstructing his bedroom set. You can relax tonight." She bit her lower lip an' gave me an' all-tellin' naughty smile before she continued, "I mean, relax until it's time for *us* to go to bed."

I loved my baby momma to damn death. I got erethang I eva wanted. A beautiful home, beautiful children, plenty of paper, an' most important, I got Michelle. She mighta called the plays but when it's all said and done I was da muthafucka who provided her wit' da pen an' da game book to write dem bitches down.

# Author Bio

Discovered by actress Drew Sidora (*The Game, Step-Up 2, White Chicks*); Ni'chelle Genovese of Norfolk, Virginia is no stranger to the pen. Even though she's like a fish in water when it comes to being in the studio or behind the mic, she has proven that she is more than just your typical artist. As a musician, Ni'chelle's main mission was to stay true to herself and beliefs. She's turned down impressive offers from Lil' Kim's Queen Bee Records as a ghostwriter and even passed on an exclusive recording contract with Bad Boy. Under the close mentoring of rapper Ice-T, Ni'chelle developed a writing style unlike any other female MC. She has since penned verses and hooks for the likes of Pink, Governor, Mike Bless, and Drew Sidora, but her heart lies in her storytelling abilities. On December 23rd, with the aid of her manager Maurice "First" Tonia, Ni'chelle self-published and released the drama-filled novel *Baby Momma*. This is the first in a three-part series that not only draws readers into its plots and ploys but spirals them into a world of passion, crime, and revenge. The novel *Baby Momma* was an instant success and caught the eye of the literary phenomenon Carl Weber. Within two months of its release, Ni'chelle Genovese was signed to an exclusive publishing deal with Carl Weber's Urban Books and is also working on a new series titled *Church Girl*. This young woman's journey has only just begun and looks to have a bright fulfilling future.

# Notes